Attention-Seeking Behavior

Attention-Seeking Behavior

A Novel

Aea Varfis-van Warmelo

Graywolf Press

First published in Great Britain by Peninsula Press, London

Published by Graywolf Press
212 Third Avenue North, Suite 485
Minneapolis, Minnesota 55401

www.graywolfpress.org

Published in the United States of America

ISBN 978-1-64445-390-2 (paperback)
ISBN 978-1-64445-391-9 (ebook)

2 4 6 8 9 7 5 3 1
First Graywolf Printing, 2026

Library of Congress Control Number: 2025950687

Cover design: Michael Salu / Vestibule Agency

Cover photo: Pexels

PART ONE

1.

You should know that when I found the body I did not scream.

On the phone, I feigned humanity. I performed the inflections of a person overwhelmed and confused, but the fact was 'no, he is definitely not breathing and there is no pulse.' I stood by him patiently as we waited for the police to arrive, hoping no dog walkers or joggers would amble near. I admit I drank my coffee, though I put my croissant in my bag for later.

The police asked their many questions and I was pragmatic in my answers. I felt like I was their colleague, my memory was so clear and my recounting so efficient. I felt like I answered in a way that suggested I was inured to horrors—humbled by them, perhaps, but no longer frightened. I said the precise time I had found the body (I'd checked), I indicated what footprints in the snow were mine and I described his original position, before I'd moved him to check for breath and pulse. They said I'd been very helpful, but I think they say that to everyone.

The man had frozen to death, this much was obvious to everyone.

I did not tell them that there was an immaculate beauty to the scene when I'd first found it, nor that I'd felt a weightless intimacy between me and this man as we'd waited for their arrival. I did not say that I felt like my life was supposed to be altered by this chance encounter, but it hadn't in the slightest. If anything, I felt like this was meant to happen to me.

You should know that on the way home I ate my croissant.

I have never told this story before.

I think of the body most often at parties, when I miss a social cue or I am strange and sharp. In the second of silence and my rude, polite smile that follows, I think of how this happened to me. That one icy morning in December, likely hours after he had slipped away privately and quietly, I was the person who found the dead man, I was the person who penetrated the secrecy of his death and now I am the one who carries it. So in cold moments, when I have not been right as a person, I know it is because I have a death inside of me. This thought is very comforting to me.

I have never told anyone about this before. There is no way to prove that it happened, but why would I lie?

•

You should know that I was born a normal child and my parents loved me as best as they could, which is all you can ask of parents.

•

You should know that when I found the body I felt sick.

The helmet was cracked but his face was concealed. Blood had pooled around him already—glassy and still, catching my headlights like a perfect mirror. His limbs were wrong.

I put my hazard lights on then called the police.

•

The second time we slept together, Normal Ben lay in my bed, soft and supine. After his practiced gesture of tucking my hair behind my ear, he told me that, on some level, I remained a mystery to him. He asked me to tell him something private, maybe something I'd never told another soul. The question was obviously rehearsed, and its obviousness was endearing.

I told him about when I found the body. I told him what he needed to know about it, I told him I cried involuntarily while waiting for the police, I told him about the enormity of feeling grief for a stranger. He asked if I was telling the truth. I asked who would lie about something like that.

•

You should know that when I found the body it was bloated beyond recognition. I smelled it before I saw it.

•

He looked disquieted. Said, 'That's a lot.' Then, 'Did it fuck you up for a bit?'

I asked if I seemed fucked up.

•

The signs are all over your face, apparently. That's where you can see it. But you can't spot it without formal training.

•

You should know that the body was warm, once.

•

Allegedly the amygdala, that small almond structure in the limbic system, the seat of your brain, knows the truth and it reveals itself in microexpressions. You can try to lie—make your gestures and expressions match how you should be moving—but apparently the amygdala knows the truth and will always give you away in a split second. Anyone could read the signs, with training.

This is not true, but many people believe it, therefore it is as true as any other fact may be.

•

Normal Ben said I seemed to be managing okay.

•

You should know that the first time I found the body I was five years old. He was lying on my bed, silent as a stopped clock.

I felt about it as I should have done and the feeling lodged itself in my stomach.

His mouth tipped open when I adjusted his head and with that motion air slipped into him. When I placed him back down on the pillow he sighed. It sounded living. I repeated the gesture twice and each time there was the same release. The air was ignorant of its passage through this object.

The moment was changed, like many are, by a thought crossing my mind—a recognition. I couldn't touch him anymore. I slid under the bed and felt his great weight hovering above me, then slept there for the three days it took the body to leave.

•

I liked Normal Ben because he made me laugh as much as I made him laugh. He cared about language as much as I do, but with a hobbyist's ease and pleasure—he only really cared about language as the natural byproduct of being devoted to laughter and flirtation.

I also liked Normal Ben's arms, which were firm and beautiful. He approached his body the same way he approached language. He didn't have a love of sports, but he did love his friends and he wanted to play whatever sports they loved, so every weekend Normal Ben would either play football, go climbing, cycle to Richmond Park or play tennis, each one until he was satisfyingly drenched in sweat. Then he and his friends would drink enough to make a day feel complete, go their separate, meandering ways and then Normal Ben would reach his flat, have an efficient shower, and sleep face-down in a room with the windows open as wide as possible. The result of these athletic habits was that Normal Ben's body was a relief map of the various ways he showed physical devotion to the people he cared about. That none of this beauty was contrived meant that when a gesture revealed a graceful muscle ridge or sinew I had an insurmountable urge to ravish him.

Normal Ben had been born as he was and he had never doubted that. His parents had loved him as best as they could, and I always suspected that his parents were better at loving than mine.

We had a hundred running jokes, but my favourite was the one where we'd start a statement with 'you should know this about me' and follow it with something either innocuous, absurd or universal. 'You should know this about me, I have to sleep a certain number of hours to survive', 'You should know this about me, there was a brief period when I was a baby where I couldn't walk or talk', 'You should know this about me, I was the guy who shot JFK and I'm worried I will kill again.'

I started it on our first date, but he made it last. As I slid out of the pub booth to head to the bathroom I announced, very seriously, 'I'm leaving my bag here, but you should know this about me: I really hate it when people I've just met steal my wallet and commit identity fraud.'

I made this stupid joke on every date and it always got a stupid laugh. That Normal Ben did not even smile helped persuade me to like him. He said, 'Okay, but you should know this about me: those are my two favourite things to do.'

At the end of our first date we stood at his bus stop as he said things about work and waking up early and I said that was fine, of course. Then in the heavy, silent beat that is the cusp of indulgence, I took his hand and ran my nail from his wrist down to the centre of his palm where I pressed just hard enough to hear him take a shallow breath, which meant I'd won.

In my bedroom I did not feel like his body would be a unique and new discovery, nor that what it would do to me was unique to him alone. I thought that, at last, he was on my level, no one could be a better person than I was here. So I stroked his neck and chest the way I did everyone else's, and he tugged at my jumpsuit the way everyone did and said the customary 'how the fuck do you take this thing off' it had been subjected to so many times before, and when I reached down and he wasn't hard yet I said 'are you Catholic or something?' between coating him in kisses and before he could answer I said 'because I give you permission to sin. In fact I insist on it, you can go to confession later' and as he started speaking I said 'I can sense your remorse! I can sense your hesitation! But it's allowed, you're allowed to get hard! You're allowed to fuck my brains out!' and his laugh was so sexy it made me grateful God made me funny and especially grateful that Normal Ben found this arousing because now successful I kissed him deeply, placed my hand around his throat and pressed against his cock which was reliably hard, pressed his jugular and asked what the worst thing about him was and before he could answer I said 'I think it's probably that you're so good looking you don't have to try very hard at all do you, people just give you things don't they' and batted away his hand as it tried to resolve my jumpsuit, 'I think it's probably that you're too secure' and he groaned and grabbed my waist, pulling me hard against him, said he fucking hated me and then I said 'what's your mother's name?' to which he flipped me over, in his swift and athletic way, so he lay on top of me and finally clamped his hand over my mouth and told me to shut the fuck up but faltered again at the jumpsuit and I wriggled smugly under him as he struggled to undress me until he rolled off, defeated, and I kissed his neck in that soft way you're supposed to and stroked his unrewarded penis and said 'tell me her name' and he sighed deeply, eyes shut and defeated, and whispered 'Maggie', and I peeled my jumpsuit off in an instant, went down on him and let him grip my hair like everyone does and then when he'd grabbed and moved me and was inside of me, eyes shut and rough, I gasped and grabbed and said 'call me Maggie' and with the briefest pause in his thrusting he said 'I have literally never met someone I wanted to fuck more and less simultaneously' and muted my laughter with his hand again and then there was hardly any talking and later when he came it was very good, it was like a punchline, it was like being understood.

Then in the pause, the space of clean up, heads on shoulders and eyes shut with deep contented breathing, a laugh rumbled through him slowly until he indulged in it fully, and after it had infected me and we were both laughing and I asked him why three times he took a deep breath and admitted, serenely, 'Her name is Sally. And yes, I am Catholic, but lapsed. And you should know this about me—I will never say my mother's name when I'm hard.'

Normal Ben never thought about language, but he knew how to play its game with me. This is why he was allowed in my bed, why I held his hand in public and why I fully surrendered to his kiss.

It didn't seem to worry him that the more a conversation is filled with laughter the less is truly said, nor that every story about my life was narratively smooth and ended with a neat conclusion. I suspected only a subconscious awareness, the slightest suspicion, of the fact that every time he laughed at my jokes he validated the character I'd invented for him and encouraged me to continue performing her.

This slight suspicion must have been what led to him asking, the second time he'd met me, for something real.

To stop that suspicion growing I had to tell him about finding the body.

That he believed me is not his fault; everyone does.

•

This notion that the amygdala secretes truth in the flickers of eyelids and the twitching of lips is almost comforting—it suggests that no matter what I say and no matter what people believe, there will always be this impenetrable lump of truth inside of me. When I'm overwrought and sick with self-hatred, I've felt it throb, hot inside my skull. I picture it as a gold and glowing gland, inhibited by some kind of blockage from secreting its truth throughout my body. I used to feel there must be a simple cure and it was my fault for not wanting it hard enough.

•

After I told him about the body, Normal Ben reclined and gazed at my ceiling for a few silent seconds. In his eyes I saw the visible outline of a corpse, my footprints in the snow, my broken breathing as I phoned the police. He pulled me into an embrace and pressed his chin to the crown of my skull. It was too intimate a gesture too soon into knowing each other. His embrace tightened. I liked it.

Everything I had told him until then led to this moment. An act of kindness I didn't deserve. I liked it so much.

•

He fell asleep shortly after, still holding me. I slipped out of his grasp to get a glass of water. On the way out of the room I was struck by how little his face was changed by sleep. Apart from a minor loosening between his brows, it seemed to me that Normal Ben's unconscious might be indistinct from his conscious.

I stood in the dark kitchen watching the shadows and light play across the brick of the opposite building, watching a neighbour pacing in his bedroom. My skin prickled where Normal Ben's arms had been wrapped around me. As I swayed in the dark my amygdala throbbed in protest. The neighbour opened his window and climbed onto the ledge. I looked away before he jumped. You should know I heard the impact.

•

This is what happened when I told Normal Ben about finding the body.

He kissed the back of my hand, our fingers interlocked, sat up and asked me to tell him something I'd never told another soul. It thrilled me. I rested on my elbow, so I could look him in the eyes, and asked 'Why do you want to know something like that?'

I wanted to offer symbols of resistance, so when I gave my confession he felt like he'd earned it.

'Well, you've interrogated me about my relationship with my mum enough, so I think it would be fair for you to tell me something too. And, I don't know, you're doing this whole mysterious and aloof thing, and it's working, obviously, I'm here. But you are actually still a bit of a mystery, and,' he shrugged, 'I guess I just want to find out what else I should know about you.'

'Isn't premarital sex enough? What more could you possibly want from me?'

'I could get that anywhere, you're not special.'

I could have felt pity for the fact that he wanted me to trust him—it could have been pathetic, but I also sensed that if I rejected him he wouldn't try again, and the integrity of that was very appealing. And a surprisingly large part of me wanted to receive his trust. I knew it would feel good, maybe better than anyone else's.

It didn't even occur to me to tell him something true.

I told him that I was walking through Battersea Park two months ago, in December, and that when I found the body I didn't scream, though I'm not sure why. I told him I'd never called 999 before and felt surprisingly nervous about it so I practiced what I had to say before dialling and then when I did I was surprised by how quickly they answered, and surprised they asked me what service I needed. I hadn't realised I would have any choice in the matter. I said police and told them where I was, what I'd found. They said they were on their way. And then I waited. I avoided Normal Ben's eye contact when I admitted to crying, very briefly, while I waited. That I'd cried because a thought had crossed my mind: I'd wondered what the body's name had been. That it seemed silly to cry over that. Then I said it was an irrelevant detail, I wasn't sure why I mentioned it. I paused. I inhaled deeply. I looked back at him when I said the police were very nice and sensible and it was reassuring actually. That after they'd asked me all their questions I walked out of the park in a daze, feeling incredibly aware of myself and my surroundings. That I came home and had to join a work call, so I did. That I felt like I was being weird on the call, but slowly remembered how to be normal. That by the time the call ended I felt like myself again. That I decided I shouldn't really talk about what had happened that morning, because I wasn't sure how I felt about it. That I still wasn't sure how I felt about it. But I was relieved to talk about it now, actually.

As he listened to me I saw him learn what he needed to know about me: that I was someone who had encountered enough pain in my life that when I experienced a new grief it touched me to the quick, joined the rest of my history, rattled me, but did not compromise my humanity. Perhaps it even deepened it. He learned that I was someone who could look after herself. He saw an opportunity to look after me too.

I said I was sorry and laughed and said 'oh god, I'm so embarrassed, that was way too heavy.' I said he probably wanted a different kind of confession, like how often I stole chewing gum from Sainsbury's. Which was 'every day, by the way. Every single day.'

He didn't laugh. He looked at me with a fold of concentration then let out a deep breath. 'That is intense, yeah,' he said, still frowning. 'That really happened?'

I laughed. 'What, like, did I make it up? Who would lie about something like that?'

'No, I don't mean… It's just. Yeah, it's a lot. Did it fuck you up for a bit?'

I gave an exaggerated shrug. 'Do I seem fucked up?'

He still refused to smile. 'Well. I mean, every day is too often to be stealing chewing gum, if we're being honest. There's something pathological about that.'

He reclined into my pillow. I was excited to watch every beat of my story replay across his face, chased by the thought of my dead mother. He looked like he was about to speak but instead pulled me into an embrace, pressed his chin into the crown of my head and said, 'No, you don't seem fucked up.'

•

As I fell asleep I thought of Normal Ben's arms. I thought of my neighbour's body. I wondered when it would be found.

•

You should know I've never told anyone I am a liar before. You should know I know the consequences of making this confession.

•

In the morning Normal Ben paused as he was putting on his shoes. He asked me why I'd said I needed the police instead of an ambulance. I tugged and undid his shoelaces with my toes and said I didn't know why, but as soon as I'd arrived it felt like a crime scene.

2.

There is no way to engage with lying without becoming embroiled in its filth. To believe a lie makes one stupid, but to detect a lie one must be suspicious, and suspicion is only attained at the cost of innocence, of believing that goodness may be real.

Lying is cheap. It is ugly, it is tacky. This is true both of liars and those who seek to understand them; trying to understand liars has a nasty habit of turning people into liars. This hasn't stopped them from trying, though.

•

We used to detect lies by making suspects chew rice, throwing them into rivers, plunging their hands into boiling water, having them take an oath, tracking their eyes, giving them a burning candle, inviting them to walk through flames, making them drink a potion, placing a hot poker on their tongue—but now we can catch liars just by looking at them. There are two forms of lie detection: verbal and non-verbal. Verbal lie detection is the kind we practice often—it is noticing that a story doesn't add up, it is asking uncomfortable questions, it is measuring the answer against what we know to be true and finding it lacking. Non-verbal lie detection is the practice of detecting the lie in the moment it is being told and it relies on being able to detect the physical giveaways that reveal a person is lying. The most famous form of non-verbal lie detection is the polygraph test, but it's such common knowledge that the polygraph doesn't work that it needs little attention. There are far more sophisticated methods of non-verbal lie detection in use now—they are adjacent to reading, and anyone can be trained in them, allegedly. This is how to catch a liar just by looking at them: you read it in their face.

•

This might sound unbelievable, but you will be persuaded if I tell it well enough.

First, you should know that feelings are felt, and that is a fact, but where they come from is more obscure. It won't surprise you that notions about the origin and function of emotions have evolved and shifted in tandem with the fads of theology, philosophy and psychology, but the discussion around this often comes to a simple question: which comes first, feeling or thought? The truth is, we don't know. There is no definitive answer to the question of whether thought creates feeling or feeling creates thought, but the dominant theory, now, is that neither thought nor feeling comes first. Both feeling and thought occur and catalyse each other with such astonishing speed they are functionally indistinct. When we perceive something, it triggers a reaction that we rationalise at the same time as our amygdala—that almond structure in our limbic system—triages emotions and distributes them throughout the body. This the truth.

But it isn't what Darwin believed. In *The Expression of the Emotions in Man and Animals* Darwin argued that emotion comes first, that 'when the sensorium is strongly excited, nerve-force is generated in excess, and is transmitted in certain definite directions,' and that we have no choice but to express it through our faces—that smiling from pleasure is a fundamental, universal experience. That the same is true of grimacing and pain, and that both of these can be credited to our animal origins. The text is divided into chapters describing the physical ways each emotion expresses itself, accompanied by a series of collages of people pulling identical grimaces, smiles and sneers. Even our most extreme emotions are represented physically, and the evidence of this is shown alongside one illustration of 'an insane woman, to show the condition of her hair'. Her hair is thick, bristly, unkempt. Darwin quotes the psychiatrist Charles Bucknell to explain that a lunatic 'is a lunatic to his finger's end'.

Darwin was wrong. He had seriously underestimated the role that habit and culture play in the formation of our facial expressions, but given his theories of facial expressions evolved as an extension of his studies into evolution, the mistake is forgivable—our startling similarities to animals could naturally extend to facial expressions, and we only know they don't thanks to extended anthropological research and mind-mapping technologies that did not exist at the time. You should know that despite this new knowledge, many people still choose to believe Darwin's theory. One of them is the psychologist Paul Ekman, and if you are someone with an academic interest in lying you will be familiar with his lifelong mission to catalogue emotions and facial expressions, and to catch liars. You will know that he is one of the reasons we can now detect lies just from looking at people's faces, and that his legacy, which spans academia, pop psychology books, and three seasons of prime-time television, deserves to be taken seriously. You will also be familiar with Ekman's definition of the lie, which is quoted in the field often: 'one person intends to mislead another, doing so deliberately, without prior notification of this purpose, and without having been explicitly asked to do so by the target'. For Ekman, and psychologists generally, intention is key—the liar wants to deceive. In a 2004 interview in which he reflected on his life's work, Ekman described the transformative experience that was discovering Darwin's theory of the universality of emotions and facial expressions during his undergraduate degree, via his mentor, the affect theorist Silvan Tomkins. The theory was lacking in evidence, because the theory is wrong, but Ekman believed in it like most people come to believe in anything: he *felt* it was right, 'but the question was,' he said, 'how do I get the evidence?'

The evidence was important, because evidence is what distinguishes a belief from a fact. Some things may be true because they are believed, but this does not make them facts. Many things may also pretend to be a fact by claiming they have evidence. A fact is only a fact when the evidence is sound. For example, Paul Ekman believed that emotions are universal, so Paul Ekman wanted to prove it is a fact that they are.

Here is a fact that is truer than others: we are capable of close to ten thousand facial gestures—from chin to forehead, ear to ear, you are holding a vocabulary of ten thousand forms of expression. Here is another fact: facial expression is acquired the same way language is: through imitation. Fact: for the first three months of its life, a baby practises the scope of its physical expression through facial contortions divorced from any intention or expression. Fact: by the end of these practice months, at the same time that a baby realises it has control of its own face, a baby will have also understood that reciprocity is the key to communication. Fact: the baby will have seen a smiling adult's face enough around incidents of kindness (a hug, a kiss, a stroking of its fine hair) that it will have come to understand the association. Fact: the baby will smile, and the adult will be delighted, will smile back, will coo, will kiss and hug. The baby will have learned that it should keep this up forever. Fact: facial expression is a habit, not an instinct. It is such a pervasive habit that it can approach something like what we think of as instinct, but this doesn't mean it is one. Fact: there are conventions, patterns and distinctions in facial expressions that correspond with the various ways people can be divided: culture, gender, sexuality, among others, can influence how you choose to use your face. This is why it can be said that facial expressions develop the same way an accent does—this is why a whole family may have different features but the same smile, this is why the way you hold your face when you are deep in thought may change after you have moved country. Fact: if it *were* instinct, your expressions would be completely involuntary. If it *were* instinct, a human who had never seen another face, human or animal, would still smile when they felt pleasure, but this is simply not what would happen. Fact: facial expressions are not universal, are not innate, and have no correlation to our emotions that isn't socially designed. Fact: it is incredibly useful to certain people to believe that none of this is true.

Paul Ekman set out to prove that facial expressions were universal and innate just like any good scientist in the 60s would do so: with a sizeable grant from the US Department of Defense. He felt the best way to demonstrate the universality of emotional expression would be to run his tests on people from what the field now calls WEIRD locations (Western, Educated, Industrialized, Rich, and Democratic) and then on people who were the exact opposite of WEIRD. If these opposites correlated, then this would confirm that expressions were innate. So, he went to the Fore people in Papua New Guinea. In the same 2004 interview, he notes that the Fore were perfect because of their distance from Western influence, and because they had no still water, 'so, of course, no mirrors, so they had never seen their own faces.' There are obviously a number of issues with all of this. The first issue needs only a casual mention: buckets, puddles, polished metal. The other issue is that Ekman was not the first Western intruder in the tribe; the Fore had in fact been visited by so many missionaries, anthropologists and tourists who wanted to engage with 'primitive' people that by the time Paul Ekman arrived the Fore were very familiar with Westerners, including Western cinema and, presumably as a result of fierce encouragement from the missionaries, Christianity. To control for this, Ekman screened out candidates he thought were too Westernised and focused on those he was certain continued to represent the social distance he desired. But my primary concern is his insistence on referring to these people as a 'Stone Age Tribe' even though they demonstrably did not live in the Stone Age but were in fact his contemporaries. This raises the question of when Ekman believes human nature began—Stone Age people smiled, sneered, looked at each other and communicated something with the shift of their eyebrows. That he believed the Fore could be entirely uninfected by the collective system of facial language we have been developing since our species became bipedal is an unavoidable shortcoming of his thinking, and the lack of empathy it takes to find it impossible these people would participate in the same world does, to say the least, give me pause.

His study was simple: he showed people staged photographs where the subjects of the photographs had been asked to perform certain facial expressions, then asked the people viewing the pictures to describe the emotion they interpreted in the face. Ekman had directed the photographs of these expressions, and then specifically selected images 'on the basis of their conformity' with how he felt emotions are depicted. Even with the odds stacked this way, the early results were unsatisfactory, so he changed his method: the Fore subjects were told a story that captured an emotion ('Happiness: His (her) friends have come, and he (she) is happy') and then asked which of three pictures best characterised the feeling present in the story. There were only six options because, in a mental leap that is characteristic of Ekman, he had come to believe there are only six forms of human emotion. Happiness, sadness, fear, disgust, anger, surprise. Any other emotions you may be capable of are in fact sub-emotions to these primary six. Over the years, Ekman actually expanded the list a number of times, ultimately concluding that pride, shame, embarrassment and excitement, are also fundamental emotions, but these are often mentioned as an afterthought, presumably because the theory of six had already been lastingly disseminated, and also, possibly, because six expressions are easier to remember than ten.

With this improved testing, the evidence was conclusive: emotional expression is universal; each person expresses joy, anger, surprise, fear, contempt, sadness, disgust, the same way; the body always knows how we really feel; our thoughts reveal themselves across our faces.

Once this concept is unfolded, accidental philosophies reveal themselves: if our bodies and faces communicate against our will, they know the truth better than we do, and truth is, therefore, a default condition, and there is, therefore, a correct and default way to be a person. Anyone who does not conform to this is concealing their feelings, and that makes them a liar. This is also why Ekman's definition revolves around the liar's intention to deceive, rather than the act of deceit; if the speaker tells their victim a lie but the victim misunderstands and fails to believe this untruth, although the world is technically unchanged and a lie has not occurred, a liar has been made nonetheless. In Ekman's philosophy, the true and detectable harm is the intention to deceive, not the harm the lie causes.

In the years since, there have been numerous attempts to recreate Ekman's research and the data he was able to gather, none of them successful. A fact without adequate evidence might revert to a belief, it might become a simple personal philosophy, but this isn't quite what happened. Over the following two decades, Ekman became an expert in deception and got to work spreading his theories. Nearly four decades after that, a research paper authored by fifty-two academics from schools of psychology, law, criminology, and communications, illustrated the damage that has been done by Ekman's and similar theorists' false science and cautioned against using it. But you don't need to know about this damage yet, you just need to know that none of this had any impact on his career and the propagation of his theories.

You can now understand why, triumphant with the belief that humans are hardwired to express themselves truthfully, he came to the conclusion that lying is simply the intention to deceive. You can understand why I think of myself at five years old, standing in the garden in my favourite dress, touched for the first time by a melancholy that doesn't belong and commanding myself to summon a smile nonetheless. According to some theories I had just discovered lying.

•

You should know that Paul Ekman follows his definition of lying with two caveats: someone who believes the lie they are telling cannot be considered a liar, because they do not have the intention to deceive, and someone who lies so compulsively they have lost a grip on both reality and a sense of their own impulse and intention, is likewise no longer a liar. One assumes that in Paul Ekman's eyes both of these characters are simply delusional, and can therefore be forgiven. I don't know if I agree.

3.

By the time I met Normal Ben I'd made peace with being a liar. The rewards significantly outweighed the costs, so I saw no reason to change anything. But this was not always the case, and this equanimity was hard-earned.

The first time I tried to fix my lying I was nineteen. I didn't know what was wrong with me exactly but I knew I was miserable and I suspected it was either a symptom of or the cause for being a liar, so I thought a professional, a therapist, would be able to help fix it. I told a doctor I was depressed and she told me I might be exaggerating what were normal feelings by giving them too much significance in my head. This was technically true, but also essentially the definition of depression, so it offered little comfort. She advised that I have a bath when I felt this way, to distract myself. On my second visit I lied and told her I'd been imagining what it would be like if I 'wasn't here anymore', and then she believed I was depressed. She referred me for six sessions of talking therapy after confirming I had no plan to kill myself in place.

I didn't have much faith in the idea of talking therapy being able to help me. In fact I felt there was a distinct irony to the idea of my treatment relying on talking, when it seemed that my being able to talk was most of the problem in the first place.

When I met the therapist—a nice woman who had an air of intelligence about her, like a piece of old furniture—I felt so embarrassed that I could only muster an intimation towards my lying. I told her that I often felt swept up in my feelings and stories, so there was a possibility I might be tempted to round my recounting too well, or to depart from the truth to explain why I feel the way I do. I suggested that maybe she should challenge me if she felt she needed to—that maybe this would be useful for me.

She said this: she obviously couldn't challenge every story of mine or I would never trust her, and instead I would have to have faith in her ability to see through me. Could I trust her to mentally note when something seemed false, and discern internally why I might lie about it?

I said that seemed acceptable to me, but obviously had no faith in her ability to read through me. Her air of intelligence dissipated.

I have to admit that I may not have been serious about curing my lying. I think I was mainly interested in being told I was correct to be miserable, that I was someone who deserved sympathy and those who found me disquieting were wrong to. I'm not sure that any of this would have been conducive to being cured. But as I was sitting in front of this woman I felt small, I felt nineteen years old and like there was something unspeakably wrong with me, that I'd been corrupted on a cellular level as some inevitable consequence of my living, my upbringing, what had been done to me, how I'd been spoken to and moulded by the world. I didn't have faith in her ability to read through me, nor did I have faith in her ability to help me, but I felt like I should try. So I told her what she needed to know:

I was born a normal child and my parents loved me as best as they could. My childhood was unusual by British standards but fairly conventional by European ones. I lived in Athens until I was sixteen where I spoke English at home, French at school and Greek everywhere else. My parents' backgrounds are needlessly confusing so I won't get into them, but they're the reason I have an English accent. Those are the basic details I feel are important for someone to know me. Being francophone was engineered by my parents, who thought it would be useful if I had an extra language, so I was placed in a French school as soon as I could walk and spoken at relentlessly by adults until I absorbed the language. I'm not sure if there's anything psychologically interesting in that, but it occurred to me recently that I didn't actually realise I was speaking or being spoken to in different languages until I was four or five, which is a little embarrassing to admit honestly, it's a pretty late age to have realised that. I was thinking about this while trying to remember the first time I felt genuine sadness—I wanted to trace the feeling through my life—and I realised it coincided with the realisation about languages. I think there were lots of reasons to be feeling that way although I don't remember it really being prompted by anything, I just remember standing in the garden in my favourite dress and having the thought, just realising that I was not happy in the way I felt I should be, which upon reflection was quite a delayed realisation actually because there were plenty of reasons for me to be unhappy at the time since I think it was around then my mother started getting sick so it makes sense, although I don't actually think any of us were aware of that sickness as a substantial and lasting thing, it just seemed kind of incidental until of course it very much wasn't, when I was seven or so and she was diagnosed and then I remember very distinctly their two faces looking down at me and saying—in English—that things might be harder at home and I'd have to show a degree of independence that hadn't been asked of me yet and I didn't know what prognosis meant but I was promised it was good and I remember feeling like I had to perform relief to them as they told me this but actually all I felt was frightened sort of sick with the feeling which was also quite new to me but also like that wasn't allowed like that feeling was the opposite of what was being asked of me so I just kept it to myself and then after that there was just less talking less standing in the garden in my favourite dress and more perfect aeons of solitude of coming home and not having my day dragged out of me of saying I was playing with my friend and being believed of buying myself hours of uninterrupted time alone so yes I'd finally discovered that awful great power of constructing my life as I wanted it to be of ferrying misinformation back and forth between my teachers and parents of telling my friends about my other better friends of hiding in the park instead of going to ballet and this won't surprise you but obviously I started stealing around then too although it wasn't significant theft so maybe it's not worth mentioning like just petty crimes you know I was hardly committing larceny at seven years old but yes anyway months and months and months of construction of saying what it took to get what I wanted of making it easy for people to leave me alone and there would be small snags moments of suspicion that would open up passage to a drip of vile guilt which began to freeze through me and for a moment I'd feel like every kindness I'd received was not deserved like whatever love the world could give me was a loan and soon it'd all be revoked but I found the perfect cure to that feeling was just another lie that it abated everything and expanded my false world until almost when I least expected it although I knew it would come eventually something would go terribly wrong there'd be a major snag and the full cold force of dread would come crashing down on me like a debt collector's knock at the door like a sickness like standing in front of shopkeepers or teachers feeling stupid and small and crying suddenly with fear more than remorse and speaking so quickly and poorly in my non-mother tongues and saying sorry I'm sorry I'm sorry please don't tell my parents please hysteria brimming and clutched at my throat until I'd say you don't understand my mother is sick and I am frightened I am alone I am scared she will die and that last part was a lie I was certain she would live and frankly in that moment I often wondered if I was faking the tears too because truly they were fear really they weren't what they were supposed to be not actual guilt or apology and honestly you know I don't know if I've ever felt guilty about lying I think I've only ever felt frightened of being found out frankly and when I was standing there looking up at these adults I could see them torn between compassion and reprimand and in the shopkeeper's case they'd simply put their hand out and I'd return my loot and thank them deeply like I truly loved them which for a moment I probably did then I'd leave the shop feeling full of death and I'd have to walk the feeling off but when it came to the teachers well they would usually write a note for me to take home that explained to my parents the reality behind my fictions and I'd put it in my bag at the bottom of it I'd shove it in there hard and then later by the bus stop I'd take my books out of my bag and then toss them back in out then back in out then in again and again until the note looked suitably and credibly crushed like it had genuinely been forgotten and not hidden and then I'd come home and be mute with fear but my day would still be mine there'd be no questions about it so I'd go to my room and slide under the bed and sleep there for three days though I'm still not sure why I did that and then a few days would pass and teachers would be dodged like a lack of eye contact disproved my existence and then I'd come home and finally they'd ask about my day in a way that suggested they knew the answer already and I could feel the phone call they'd received reverberating through the house and I always wondered how they'd even spoken to each other my parents and teachers who mostly didn't speak the same languages but evidently they'd managed well enough and the crumpled note would be revealed and it being allegedly forgotten was apparently worse than it being hidden although I doubt they meant that and my world would crumble and I'd sob with hysteria at the throat again now spilling out and heaving I'm sorry I'm sorry I'm sorry it won't happen again I'm sorry I love you I'm sorry I promise I promise I really promise never again I won't do it again I won't, but I did. I simply always did.

I told her those were the facts as I was thinking of them that day. On another day I would probably tell that story very differently. I did not tell her about the bodies.

She asked me if I'd lied about anything. I said only the larceny, 'I actually committed larceny all the time.'

There was no diagnosis because she wasn't medically qualified to give one, which seriously disappointed me. But she said that there was a lot for us to talk through in our five remaining sessions and if I was willing to work very hard in that time and devote myself to truth then we could make some real progress together. She asked if I was willing to be brave, because this work would require bravery. I nodded while I sobbed, thanked her for listening to me and not thinking I was a lost cause. I said yes, yes, I am willing to work hard, I am willing to be honest, I am, thank you.

Outside her office I found the massacred corpse of someone who had leapt from the roof, their skull burst open like a pomegranate.

I went home and stayed there for a week, then never spoke to her again.

•

The prevailing theory is that pathological lying is not a distinct psychological disorder of its own, but rather the symptom of a larger condition—likely some kind of personality disorder. I didn't know this when I was nineteen, but in retrospect it is clear that I was operating under such an assumption: that my unhappiness and my lying were powerfully linked in some way. But I slowly realised that this was not as true as I had thought. At the end of that week of forced isolation I emerged and, unsteadily, returned to my life. I showed interest in the people around me, listened sympathetically. Asked personal questions and always said 'only if you're comfortable sharing' after them. I used a tone that suggested I cared about the answer. I did, but not for the reasons they thought. I developed a knack for understanding what people wanted from me. I gave it to them. They thought I was a good person for it. I sometimes believed this too, which made the lying easier.

I looked at other liars with derision and invented sophisticated categories and rules to distinguish myself from them. People who lied about having cancer and attached themselves like leeches to other people's sympathy and kindness, which manifested both emotionally and often financially, were not simply liars: they were scammers. People who fabricated university degrees, who doctored official documents and sick notes, were not liars but fraudsters. These people were so divorced from reality and so self-deluded that I honestly found it hard to think about them too long without second-hand embarrassment overwhelming me. I wasn't like them, I was a liar; I used language to adjust the world's course so I could be treated how I deserved to be: with respect, with kindness. I kept a steady foot in reality and refused to fall victim to myself.

Eventually, I was content. Content—not exactly happy, but I had come to understand that I had a proclivity towards melancholy that was incurable, frankly, because it wasn't pathological. I realised this was simply who I was: my happiness was not as happy as others' happiness, but that this state was not as devastating as I had been led to believe it should be. I learned to treat sadness with familiarity and affection, to massage it out like it was a cramp. Life seemed liveable this way. I also realised that in this contented state I still lied relentlessly. I lied for fun, I lied to flirt, I lied to steal, I lied to get sympathy, I lied to hurt, I lied for privacy, I lied to be treated with respect, I lied simply because I could.

I came to realise that this was my lot in life: that I was a liar, not because of some larger disorder, but in the same way that any personality trait is an inheritance from the world that made you.

The benign melancholy I had befriended was distinct, however, from the acute and devastating meltdowns that

I experienced when a lie of mine crumbled, or when I felt that I couldn't keep the performance up. I would have to take shelter from these meltdowns and survive them as if they were a hurricane. But they seemed like rational responses to a situation of my own making. It seemed, therefore, that the only way to avoid these depressive spirals was to avoid being caught out in my lies. In other words, I had to become a better liar, so this is what I did.

4.

IF A FACE INVOLUNTARILY REVEALS the emotional landscape of the person behind it, then someone skilled in reading faces will be able to determine what feelings the speaker is having simply by looking at them. The question: if a person can adopt a false facial expression to conceal the real emotion they are feeling, can their masking fully conceal their true feeling? The real answer is yes, the Ekman answer is no.

The Ekman answer is that the face will always reveal its truth in small glimpses—when we experience an emotion, 'muscles on the face begin to fire involuntarily'; the emotion's corresponding expression will always emerge. You may have cheated on your wife and, when confronted, conceal your fear at being discovered by feigning anger, furrow your brow and shout that she's being crazy, and in the process reveal, for almost exactly either a quarter or a half of a second, an upturned brow, a downward grimace: the expressions of fear. This is according to Ekman's philosophy. Also according to Ekman, someone skilled at reading faces would be able to notice the glimpses—which are called 'micro expressions'—of these incongruous emotions and would know to press beyond your first defence, to ask where you really were when you had to 'work late'. Your wife will also likely call bullshit, but her method has no scientific basis, which further demonstrates her irrationality.

The second question is how one becomes skilled at reading facial expressions. There is in fact an easy way to do it, for a few hundred dollars, but first you should know about the FACS.

During the research in Papua New Guinea, Ekman and Silvan Tomkins, the theorist who had first prompted Ekman's move into Darwinism, were examining photographs of tribespeople pulling different facial expressions. Tomkins moved through the images and, according to Ekman, was able to read these faces with astonishing precision, from correctly assessing the subjects' emotional states down to detecting whether they came from cultures that were pacifist or violent. When Ekman asked him how it was possible for him to know this, Tomkins indicated the exact face pulls, down to the exact muscle, that revealed this all to him. This made an impression on Ekman. His duty was clear to him: 'I had to develop a tool, a scientific tool, so that anybody can measure and get the kind of information Tomkins did.' So Ekman set out to create the FACS, the Facial Action Coding System, a taxonomy of every facial gesture and expression the face is capable of, and the emotion it was representing. He broke the face down into each muscle that composes it and then codified each of the ten thousand movements our face is capable of. The FACS assigns each facial gesture and muscle twitch a number, which can be paired with a letter from A to E to score the intensity of the expression on a scale of 'trace' to 'maximum'. For instance, someone concentrating strongly while watching television would be 4C (lowered brow, marked or pronounced) + 55 (head tilt left). After eight years, the FACS was completed, and came to serve dual functions: a taxonomy that enables careful annotation of the face and its motions, and, also, a dictionary of facial expression.

By this point, Ekman had experienced a great deal of derision from his peers. His work had been widely challenged, particularly by the anthropologist Margaret Mead, whose own research suggested that facial expressions are the result of culture and not nature and referred to Ekman's work as 'improper anthropology'. Incidentally, while making the FACS, Ekman announced there was compelling evidence that there were in fact *seven* universal emotions, and expanded the list to include contempt.

Mead's contention with Ekman's work was that a concentration on biology would be weaponised by fascists. In her autobiography, she wrote that she and her husband, Gregory Bateson, also an anthropologist, had decided to put a pause to their research into the biological causes for human behaviour in 1935, in the face of Nazism and Social Darwinism; '[We] recognized that there were dangers in such a formulation because of the very human tendency to associate particular traits with sex or age or race, physique or skin color, or with membership of one or another society, and then to make invidious comparisons based on such arbitrary associations. [...] It seemed clear to us that the further study of inborn differences would have to wait upon less troubled times.' I discover this quote from Mead's autobiography in Ekman's afterword to an edition of Darwin's *The Expression of the Emotions in Man and Animals*, where Ekman seeks to explain why he, 'an unknown scientist half the age of these luminaries', had faced such resistance to his work. He cites Mead's reluctance and says he sympathises with her concerns, and credits her for her foresight of the abuse of science, but that she had 'more than postponed' the necessary study. He paints a picture where cultural relativists such as Mead maintained some kind of tyranny over the field of psychology for the first half of the twentieth century, forcing scientists to find more evidence that humans are entirely the result of nurture rather than nature—that during this era of science 'there was no acknowledged limit to how much human nature could be reconstructed by changing the environment. Change the state, educate the parents, modify child-rearing practices and we would have a nation of renaissance men and women.' In any case, says Ekman, Mead's concerns were misplaced when it comes to modern uses of Darwinism, since the theory of evolution (which none of the characters in this drama have any contention with and agree upon, I am happy to report) is an anti-racist belief—if all humans share the same ancestor then notions such as eugenics, or that the white race has more advanced origins, have no scientific basis. Although this assessment of Darwinism is technically correct, it is surprising how divorced it is from the reality of how Darwinism was interpreted in the early twentieth century, and of the actual tyranny that was occurring at the same time. Social Darwinists were technically wrong in their interpretation of Darwin's theories (the phrase 'survival of the fittest' wasn't even written by Darwin), but this didn't prevent the belief from developing into a genocide. Facts are very often irrelevant when confronted with the force of belief—Mead and Bateson were right to say that science can be manipulated to serve bias, whether the interpretation of the science is accurate or not. It is genuinely hard to understand why Ekman's priority is to gripe about the field of psychology's narrow focus during this phase of history, especially because it is one of the few instances where Ekman seems to value accuracy so highly. But it becomes easier to understand why Ekman would be keen to ignore how science is misapplied if we take the FACS's future into account.

The FACS is a taxonomy and a taxonomy cannot be evil, or kind, or sympathetic, or forgiving, unless, of course, it is used by someone with a certain philosophy. When the FACS is used by someone who believes that facial expressions are direct representations of your true feelings, the FACS can read your mind, the FACS is a lie detection tool.

5.

There were things Normal Ben didn't need to know.

For instance, when I first met him, Normal Ben was one of a dozen people I was dating. This number and my definition of 'dating' are flexible, but at the time my life was lacking in traditional structure: I worked a handful of freelance jobs with varying devotion and income, lived in a three-bedroom flat where one room seemed incapable of retaining a tenant for more than six months, and was also on temporary-but-likely-to-become-permanent leave from a master's degree because I was incapable of meeting any deadlines. I'd credited the latter to a fictional family crisis and had received a year-long reprieve from the university. At the time it seemed like either my jobs, my flat, my prospects—or possibly all three simultaneously—could collapse at any moment, and I wasn't entirely sure how I'd cope if they did. The degree I told myself I could take or leave, but the possibility of failing at something I'd once been set on did make me queasy and I predicted would inflict some lasting psychological damage when I would be forced to confront the full reasons for my failure. The flat was shockingly affordable for London but our landlord was growing impatient with the constant flatmate rotation and clearly suspected that Thomy and I, the flat stalwarts who were also relentlessly pleasant and good-smelling, were somehow driving people away and during an inspection he'd threateningly observed that the flat could easily attract wealthier tenants, perhaps people who worked in marketing, or even Australians. I never boasted to our landlord that one-third of my income came from working in something like marketing myself, because I doubted he would find this more appealing than someone who earned three-thirds of their income from working in marketing, but also because I inexplicably cared about my landlord thinking I was cool. So I'd told him I was a writer, which at the time was not entirely true, and not at all wise. But the jobs—the thought of losing even one of them was enough to ruin my mood so thoroughly that I'd have to repair it gently and affectionately, often by feeding myself expensive strips of ham, like I was coaxing a feral cat out from under a car, and when the ham failed I would turn to sex.

•

I found dating incredibly stabilising. After the end of a tumultuous relationship I emerged blinking into the light and discovered that real pleasure was not monogamy, real pleasure was sticking your fingers in other people, so dating developed a rhythm that became one of the clearest structures to my life. I would go on two dates a week with different people, and then I would see these people once again two weeks later, after which I began to lose interest no matter how nice they were, and would find a replacement for them within hours. The aim was to have sex on all of these dates. I liked the process of getting to know new people, especially people I disliked on principle because of their job, politics or taste, so I could understand a psychological framework that seemed foreign to mine, but I mostly liked the process of becoming known to new people and practicing different parts of my personality—displaying the worst parts and seeing how far I could go until they pulled back. I was mildly antagonistic and mocking to everyone and I liked dragging people down to this level, where I could disarm them of whatever front they were putting on and make them admit to their embarrassing desire to be seen as cool, clever or successful. I told them stories about my life that were either significantly exaggerated or entirely invented, would make declarations about my habits or beliefs that were fictional and often painted me as someone who had principles, even though I often worried I didn't, and then I would tell them what I guessed their childhood had been like, most of the time correctly. This game would then spill over into our sex, which was fun, respectful if slightly vindictive, and devoid of any unnecessary affection. I realised that having fun with someone was a lot like liking them and being liked back, but better.

I met most of these people using three dating apps, which I maintained and monitored with remarkable verve in a way that unpleasantly suggested to me I had some project manager potential, although I had no idea how to include this revelation on a CV. I liked that I could pick up my phone at any given moment and have someone to talk to, I liked that dating profiles offered an insight into how people perceived themselves and what they thought was most attractive about themselves, and I liked how everyone did their best not to be boring. It was also a place where almost everyone lied, mostly very badly, and I felt faintly proud of them for trying. More often than not I found the men embarrassing and desperate and the women aloof and hot, both offering very different but equally rewarding challenges. Normal Ben, however, had an interesting inclination towards feminine aloofness. I came across him about a year after I'd started using dating apps. The first picture on his profile was of him with his arms crossed and a pint of lager on the table in front of him. It was taken on 35mm film with flash on, so the contrast was high and the colours undersaturated, making his hair look the same colour as his light brown T-shirt. He looked introspective, clever and quite beautiful, like a 19th century painting of a poet or a landowner's scholarly son. I was instantly drawn to him and felt a small but genuine fear that he wouldn't like my profile. This rarely happened because my profile was so openly solicitous, but when it did I would feel more hurt than I care to admit. So this fear stayed like a stitch in my lower ribcage as I scrolled to the next picture, which was a selfie where he was brushing his teeth. He looked hot in it and experience had taught me that men who took good selfies were sluts, so my affection grew. He'd listed his profession as ‘emails’, had pictures with friends and one in a graduation gown where he was mid-blink. What I could see of the university suggested it was fairly old, maybe Scottish, maybe Bristol, but thankfully not Oxbridge. I couldn’t find anything genuinely embarrassing about his profile—he just looked remarkably normal and well-adjusted, and the ease with which he carried these traits was incredibly sexy.

I replied to his toothbrushing picture with ‘only nine out of ten dentists recommend this’ and he replied ‘I do it to spite the tenth’, so our first date was two days later.

•

On the date he wore a faded grey T-shirt that was slightly frayed at the collar, the rip touching the soft of his neck where his pulse thrummed gently. I imagined that spot slick with sweat, I imagined kissing it, I imagined watching his pulse stop as he slept. I told him a joke and he laughed. I imagined kissing it again.

•

On the date I told him about how my mother used to tell me the plots of her favourite films and become so moved by her recounting that she’d cry while describing the denouement, I told him that when I moved to the UK my English accent meant no one realised I was foreign so everyone interpreted my wide-eyed confusion about things like Greggs or the Wombles as stupidity or performed eccentricity, I told him we'd moved to the UK because my mother had died but this wasn't a big deal and didn't require psychotherapy or any further questions, I told him about how seriously I'd taken my undergraduate degree and that this devotion was reflected in my grades but not my professional prospects, I told him I didn't know why but I didn't like it when people called me by my name, I told him that I was the one who maintained the social equilibrium between my flatmates and I thought this earned me the right not to clean the bathroom, he told me he barely remembered anything earlier than his seventh birthday, he told me he attributed this to the fact that his birthday present that year was a Game Boy Advance and that he'd been so, so happy about this that he thought the explosion of joy obliterated any earlier memories, he told me he thought it was worth it, he told me he had no siblings but had two lots of cousins he'd grown up with and he loved them all like siblings, he told me he was closest with the cousin who was six months younger and bizarrely had the same name as him, he told me he did think a lot less of his aunt for having chosen that name, which isn't even a family name, he told me he was paralytically frightened of mice and didn't know why, he told me this extended to *Tom and Jerry* and that he rooted for the cat each time but he could never remember its name, I told him he had a fifty percent chance of getting the name right each time so why not try, he told me he didn't like those odds, I told him I had to go to the bathroom and that he should know I hate being robbed by strangers, he told me I should know that robbing strangers is his favourite thing to do, I told him I'd be back in a minute, in a minute I told him he had to tell me why his last relationship had ended, he told me his last relationship ended because she fell out of love with him, he told me 'so you should know that I'm the kind of person you can fall out of love with', I told him that wasn't up to him to decide, I told him I bet his relationship had lasted just under five years, he told me I was right, I told him he hadn't asked but he should know my ex was probably the worst person in the world and I'd never known I could truly hate a person until that relationship, I told him that my ex's paintings were derivative of Lucian Freud's but my ex was so intellectually and creatively shallow he couldn't consider a judgement-free form of abjection so everything he painted was a process of humiliating its subject rather than revealing it, I told him I'd refused to be painted, I told him my ex had done a small sketch of me sleeping anyway, I told him I am an ugly sleeper, he told me I couldn't know that for a fact but maybe he could let me know and then he said nothing but smiled slightly, he told me he didn't know who Lucian Freud is but my ex sounded like a cunt, I didn't tell him that I knew he wouldn't know who Lucian Freud is and I'd been trying to embarrass him to establish intellectual dominance, he told me his best friend's little sister is a painter too and he's never liked her so maybe painters are the problem, he told me he thought all creatives were kind of weird in some way and in love with their weirdness, I asked him if that applied to me, he told me he wasn't sure yet but he was looking forward to finding out, he told me he had work the next day, I told him that was okay, he told me he had to wake up early, I told him that was fine, he told me he wanted to kiss me, I told him he could, he should.

•

I did something similar with someone else two days later, but it wasn't as good. I didn't tell him that.

•

Besides the thrill of sex and new people, my favourite thing about the dating was the sense of solitude it gave me. I really valued and nourished my loneliness by spending Saturday mornings enjoying a mild hangover and reflecting on the sex of the past week. I liked to think about how I was the only person who knew everything there was to know about me. I liked to visualise this idea like it was a Venn diagram where I sat completely alone in the centre, and I loved the feeling this gave me so much that I would try to conjure as many configurations of it as I could; I imagined two people I'd fucked sitting next to each other on the tube, entirely unaware that they had me in common, I imagined my flatmates asking each other where I was that night and neither knowing the answer, I imagined another fuck coming across a poem of mine in some anthology in a Waterstones. The odds of this last one were literally zero given my proclivity for dating people who seemed largely uninterested in—and perhaps incapable of—reading, paired with the fact that none of my poetry had appeared in books that would be sold in Waterstones. But I especially liked this fantasy, for obvious reasons.

Each new fantasy would reward me with the renewed discovery of my isolation and potential for self-determination and I would savour this feeling like sucking on a perfectly hard and sour sweet.

•

Sometimes these fantasies would accidentally veer into an image of two people I'd slept with engaging in conversation and discovering their mutual connection. They'd laugh and idly compare their experiences with me, realise they'd met me in the same week, and even this would tickle them. Then one would cautiously ask the other if they'd found me a little… you know, odd? And the other would say yes, they had, but this was probably on account of my cousin having died the week before. Then the other would pause, a grey veil falling across their face, and they'd say that this didn't add up—we'd discussed family and I never mentioned a dead cousin. Then they'd both realise that the only thing they actually knew about me was that I was a liar.

The first time this image came to me I was at a train station in South East London the morning after a date. On the platform, I'd sheltered from the rain in one of those archaic and useless phone booths, and shuddered at the thought of this imaginary conversation, a familiar fear seeping through me as a train screeched closer. Through the filthy glass of the phone booth I watched a man step forward and slip near the edge of the platform. He vanished beneath the train before I could gasp. I felt much better.

•

Eventually, all Normal Ben and I would do was talk (everywhere, in pubs, near the pond, in his car, on the tube over the sound of screaming gears, on WhatsApp for most of each day, at parties with his friends, at the airport as he ate two sandwiches, at the beach that one time, on the walk home, on the phone as I cried, a few times in restaurants, in his mother's living room, in my father's living room, in the garden as I smoked, on the balcony as I smoked, at the bus stop as I smoked, in my bedroom as he cried, and of course in shops, marvelling at the girth of leeks) but at first all we really did was fuck.

He slotted into my two-week system but I kept seeing him past the second date—once he'd heard about the body and met it with kindness it felt like we'd entered some kind of contract. So for several months we would meet every two weeks in a pub of his choice, drink to the brink of drunkenness and then go to whichever bed of ours was nearest. Whether we were in a pub or bed I would ask him prying questions about his childhood, time at university and previous relationships, and he shared almost everything without any hesitation.

I felt like I'd grasped his psychological architecture within hours of meeting him so I was constantly surprised by how much I enjoyed his company and how much I wanted to see him, despite the lack of challenge he presented, and despite how uncomplicated the emotional circumstances of his life had been. But I remained interested. I ascribed this to the fact that his primary dialect was irony, and that he was conscious of the banality of his life and therefore knew to tell his stories in a way that anticipated my expectation and satirised both of us, me for finding his life easy and him for having had an easy life. This doubling, the act of self-conscious narration, was incredibly similar to what I did, so in a very simple but significant way, Normal Ben and I got along. And that my predictions about his life were always correct meant that Normal Ben's predictability was a permanent endorsement of how perceptive and intelligent I am, so I could sink blissfully into the emotional performance of listening sympathetically to stories from an average life while feeling good about myself.

Two months in, lying in bed, I asked him to describe his dead dog to me and when he started with 'well, I'm glad you asked because obviously, as I'm sure you've guessed, she was the best dog in the world', I already felt a surge of arousal that I had to spend by kissing the inside of his wrist. I knew the story would slide through vignettes about the dog sleeping next to him as he watched TV, her visible and near-human intelligence and empathy, and at least one story about her doing something disgusting, like eating a dead rat. If he'd been any other person at this point I would have told him my predictions and mocked him for the eulogy, but by then I didn't need to, because he knew I was thinking it. By bypassing this urge I allowed myself to be genuinely moved by his phenomenal dead dog, and this miraculous display of empathy perplexed and fascinated me and, crucially, made me like myself so much that it turned me on, so this is how teasing out Normal Ben's stories about his greatest and comparatively frivolous miseries began to constitute a kind of foreplay. As he told me about his dog named Radar I kissed his neck and pressed against him but before I could get him hard he grabbed my wrist and said, 'Stop getting turned on by my dead dog,' to which I could only say, 'I can't help it, she just sounds so fucking hot,' and fuck him as I repeated how incredible this dog must have been.

Conversely, I suspected that he found identical satisfaction in thinking of me as interesting. I had no doubt that when his friends asked what I was like the first word he would use was 'arty', and I knew that he would wield this word semi-sarcastically in an attempt to pre-empt what they would actually think of me (that I was posh and arrogant), but I also knew that it gave him a sense of fullness and satisfaction to think of me as someone complex, someone foreign, creative and nasty. So for every question I asked about his simple life, he would ask me what it was like growing up in Greece, how I'd felt about my mother's death, what it was like to be published and if I ever felt insecure. He'd often ask these as he was making me wet so more often than not my answers were 'hot', 'sad', 'good' and 'never' and then he'd spit in my mouth. In the moment, these answers were entirely satisfying—the erotic charge for him was that I was someone to whom these questions could be asked, and that the rest was up to his imagination made everything so much better for both of us.

6.

Science is public but science is also private—although Ekman claimed his intention in making the FACS was simply to create a tool that would benefit the scientific and larger academic community, this claim is difficult to reconcile with the amount of money Ekman has made from it and his associated lie detection theories.

In 1985, a decade before he dismissed Margaret Mead's concerns about the misuse of science, Ekman published a mass-market psychology book, *Telling Lies: Clues to Deceit in the Marketplace, Politics, and Marriage*, in which he expresses a very different sentiment. In fact he admits that he was disquieted by the various appeals he was receiving from law enforcement and intelligence agencies, American or otherwise, to instruct them on lie detection: 'I was not pleased with this interest, afraid my findings would be misused, accepted uncritically, used too eagerly. I felt that non-verbal clues to deceit would not often be evident in most criminal, political, or diplomatic deceits.' The book's success only bolstered these solicitations and, at some point, for some unknown reason, Ekman yielded. A second edition of the book, published seven years later, includes a chapter on the process of teaching his lie detection methods to law-enforcement and secret service agents. Ekman says that he entered these training sessions apprehensively. Given that he felt that non-verbal deception clues weren't likely to appear in the course of these people's work, the first thing to do was to disabuse them of their confidence in their own skills—to show them how challenging this really is. So the training began with a lie detection test that practically every member failed. Ekman was steeled for his students to challenge him on this—accuse him of running a useless test that was irrelevant to the sorts of lies they encountered day-to-day. Perhaps in this moment of apprehension he thought of Alan Lomax Jr., who, during one of Ekman's lectures at the American Anthropological Association, stood up and shouted that Ekman was a fascist. Instead, the officers he was training were invigorated—they welcomed the challenge and the chance for improvement. 'They were more courageous than my academic colleagues when I have offered them the same opportunity to learn,' he says. After this point, his work increasingly pivoted away from the academic space and further into this realm of application.

By Paul Ekman's own definition, we don't know if he's a liar because we don't know if he believes what he sells. It is very easy to imagine that at some point, in the face of enormous criticism, he realised what he was peddling was false, but it was too late to turn back. It's even possible to imagine that he knew he was doing something wrong in Papua New Guinea when he showed subjects only three pictures instead of six, when he directed their answers with stories. But you should know that it's just as easy to believe the opposite. In 1987, two years after *Telling Lies* had been published and presumably when Ekman was receiving increased calls away from academia, he wrote an introspective essay called 'A Life's Pursuit' where he reflected on his devotion to the study of the face and lie detection. It begins with the confession that the 'crucial event' that triggered this all was that his mother killed herself when he was fourteen years old. The following year Ekman was expelled from high school and, by some fluke of the education system at the time, he was able to begin an undergraduate degree in psychology. It was during this degree, when studying suicidal patients, that he first became interested in the idea of lie detection—when the thought crossed his mind that if you could tell when a suicidal patient was lying about no longer wanting to harm themselves, you could save them from themselves. In *Telling Lies* he describes studying the footage of a patient named Mary as she persuades her doctor to give her a weekend pass away from the psychiatric institution she is being treated in. Mary has every intention of taking her life once she is granted this pass. Ekman and his research colleagues studied the footage of this interview for hours to find something that could have betrayed her intentions—something future psychiatrists could detect in their patients. Eventually, 'In a moment's pause before replying to her doctor's question about her plans for the future, we saw in slow-motion a fleeting facial expression of despair.' This confirmed his theory of 'non-verbal leakage'—that the face will give us away. You can understand why he wanted to believe this.

Because we are human beings and this is what human beings do, we have license to take the evidence available to us and imagine Paul Ekman's inner life however we like. The world is a better place by one if we imagine a fourteen-year-old boy's relentless attempts to save his mother rather than a pseudoscientist eager to sell his grift.

But many conflicting things may be true at once, and regardless of Ekman's motivations, there was a point where his work moved beyond any noble hopes and into a seedier realm. He continued to work with the FBI, the CIA and the TSA; he started to sell FACS-based courses on how to read non-verbal cues and become lie detectors in hours to the public for just a few hundred dollars. He helped design the TSA's security programme for American airports, a post-9/11 terrorism-prevention initiative. The concept of this programme was directly based on FACS—TSA agents were trained to identify micro-expressions to help identify potential terrorists in airports. You should know that every year, TSA agents stop approximately 30,000 people, 80% of whom are not white, 1% of whom are then arrested, none for terrorism. The programme is widely criticised, by academics and civil rights campaigners, for the fact that it actually does nothing more than allow TSA agents to racially profile passengers under the claim that it is scientifically backed. In 2015, Ekman published a blog post defending the programme, and the language he uses here is jarringly different from his earlier academic and commercial work—here he writes about trying to catch 'real bad guys' and how critics have to 'get back to the real world', and then, in a strange move for a man defending a programme accused of facilitating racial profiling, he says that criminals trying to sneak through airport security will undoubtably show the suspicion-inducing signs of stress because the reward for success places so much pressure on them, whether that reward is 'money or 72 virgins'.

This world that Ekman had entered, where research is readily welcomed by those who need solutions, and where data is hazy and unreliable, is well-populated. One of Ekman's colleagues in it is Dan Ariely. Ariely and Ekman differ in that, although they both came to this via the field of psychology, Ariely's focus narrowed into behavioural science, specifically behavioural economics. You will struggle to find anyone more cynical, more convinced of people's laziness, stupidity, greed and general malevolence than a behavioural scientist. Ariely's work largely boils down to providing a familiar answer to a familiar question: he argues that people do not make decisions based on rational thought but are instead persuaded into making choices through subconscious motivations and, essentially, instinct. The people inclined to agree with the findings of behavioural economists are people who see themselves in the results: they are lazy, stupid, greedy and generally malevolent people. They are also, quite often, policymakers. The result of this kind of cynical philosophy is putting graphic pictures of burst arteries or grey lungs on cigarette packets instead of implementing smoking bans; it is police forces cracking down on small crimes by increasing racially motivated stop-and-searches because Malcolm Gladwell wrote that broken windows in an area induce people into greater criminality.

After finding success in his commercial writing about irrationality, Ariely moved into studying and writing about dishonesty. Here he put forward the idea that people are most often honest because of a concept called 'self-concept maintenance'—a cost-benefit analysis where, in a situation where it is beneficial to lie, a person will measure the benefit of lying against the cost of being truthful and the risk of being caught, and that in most cases, when a person elects to be honest, it is a process of simple moral economics: they've decided that being found out would be more damaging than the lie would be rewarding. In the instances where lying is worth it, the final loss is the ability to perceive oneself as honest; for Ariely, we are honest simply for the purpose of seeing ourselves as honest. If you think it is a hollow conscience that is being proposed here, where people are vacuous, impressionable and moral purely for the sake of performance, you are not wrong. But it is possible that Ariely is truthfully reporting his own experience of the world. You should know that in 2021, a team of vigilante data scientists who call themselves Data Colada and are dedicated to fact-checking social scientists, proved that Ariely had falsified, and perhaps even entirely invented, the data in one of his studies—a study into whether including an honesty declaration at the start of a car insurance form could subtly induce people to be more honest about their mileage. The results showed, overwhelmingly, that the answer was yes. When the data was revealed to be false, Ariely accepted that mistakes had been made but denied any part in making them. Although Ariely's claim was upheld after a three-year investigation by the university where he is a professor, the doubt has cast a heavy shadow on his name that is unlikely to lift, not least because of the irony.

It is curious, when wading into the field of behavioural sciences, to discover that it shares the same constructs of fact and fiction as the rest of our normal, unscientific world: the possibility of something being true means that it might be true. Ariely's downfall wasn't because of the dubiousness of his claims, or how dubiously the data may have been sourced, but because the data was found to be false. Ekman, too, like the rest of us, benefits from the hazy perimeters of truth; the data that supports his science may be imprecise and impossible to replicate, but his claims stand because data exist. Challenging this science is like calling a bluff: you either need evidence, or a confession from the liar.

You should know that PIXAR and other animation studios use the FACS to animate expressive digital faces. The very nature of the FACS means it can be computerised easily. This is also why a number of startups have adopted the FACS to develop lie-detecting AI software that is used to screen job candidates, and refugees or asylum-seekers trying to cross the EU's borders. You should know that in 2018 the National Institute of Standards and Technology published a report stating that every single face-scanning

AI had a racial bias and struggled with correctly analysing a non-white face.

But this shouldn't be a problem—we know that facial expressions are universal and they transcend any of these challenges.

We have proof.

7.

You should know I felt no remorse about lying to my employers. I know hardly anyone does, but I felt perhaps less remorse than the average person.

When I met Normal Ben, my primary income came from working for a small PR company three days a week for a slim salary, my secondary income was from running monthly poetry workshops for the elderly, and I mostly found myself lying to these two employers to make time for myself or for my third and final strand of employment, which was unpredictable, complicated and difficult to define but came the closest to being creatively and intellectually satisfying.

I started working for the PR company about a year before I met Normal Ben. For some time before that, I'd been obsessed with the idea of gaining control over my time. Because of my notion of myself as a writer I believed any job I did was, ultimately, a waste of time, and after a series of physically and emotionally demanding jobs where I'd felt watched every second of the day, I was convinced that something had to change. Not only were these jobs a waste of time, but they destroyed whatever time surrounded them by leaving me mentally paralysed at the end of each day. So I needed a job that was less tiring and where, crucially, I had agency. I was convinced that if I wasn't being supervised constantly and if I had this agency, then I'd be able to loosen my synapses a bit and allow space for more productive enquiries to play through my mind in tandem with whatever useless work I did to pay my rent. In other words, I needed an office job.

This posed a serious challenge because I seemed incapable of getting myself an interview anywhere, no matter how much I embellished facts in my cover letters and CV. When I got an interview for this PR company I was ecstatic but then I realised that although the contents of the email weren't technically unusual, it was sent by the company's CEO and not some assistant running recruitment, and the final sentence of the email was 'It will be lovely meeting you...' before the CEO's signature, which hyperlinked to a misspelled version of the company website. This obviously set off some alarm bells, the ellipsis above all, but by that point in my job search I felt it made sense that the only place that would consider hiring me would be somewhere that seemed like a scam. I confessed this thought to a friend who told me that what I was experiencing was called impostor syndrome, but then I had my interview and it was confirmed that what I had been experiencing was common sense.

The CEO was a woman in her early fifties named after a Shakespearean heroine, so I will be calling her Desdemona. My interview with Desdemona took place in the restaurant of a posh hotel that immediately made my best clothes look cheap. There is no way that Desdemona didn't think my clothes looked cheap, but she didn't mention it. Instead she told me about the company, which still sounded fake, why she'd founded it and what I would be doing for it, as if I had the job already. She barely asked me about any of my professional experience because the only questions she seemed interested in asking me were about my upbringing, and she was especially interested in hearing about why I spoke the languages I do, how I felt about the cultural interplay of my upbringing, and what my parents had done for work. This last question was Desdemona's attempt to confirm my class status and although I knew it would benefit me to lie, there really was no way to—rich people knew how to identify these markers faster and better than anyone else and I knew that my answer wouldn't actually reveal anything, it would just confirm her suspicions. So I told her the truth, that they were translators, and she said, 'I see. Not very lucrative… It must have given you character.' We only ordered coffees and she ordered hers black with the milk on the side. When the coffees arrived she instantly said, 'Now there is a real problem here…' and the real problem was that her coffee cup was so full there no space for her to pour in her milk. I said, 'Oh no, you'll have to take a sip to make some room' and she looked at me like I had said a slur. She beckoned the waiter back and had them make her a new, smaller coffee. As we waited for her new coffee to arrive I didn't drink mine out of respect and she said, apropos of nothing, 'Your parents must have loved you very much' and I said, 'Of course, as much as they were able to, yes' and she said, 'They must have done, to have given you so many languages...' and then she told me about growing up between France and London and how she thought boarding school was tantamount to child abuse. 'A child must be cuddled...' she said, and I nodded and said my childhood had not been lacking in cuddles, it was true. I asked her sympathetic questions about her upbringing and then said celebratory things about multiculturalism, although her being from two Northern European countries didn't seem all that impressive, least of all being French and English, a combination that indicated to me that her ancestors' ambition was limited to crossing a narrow body of water. At one point she asked me where my grandparents were from, which is the precursor to a certain type of middle-aged European engaging in amateur eugenics, and I briefly wondered if grandparents should become a protected characteristic. That my grandparents were white South Africans and Albanians complicated things, given the fact that I couldn't exclude the possibility that she could be racist and xenophobic and therefore likely torn between liking and disliking me as a result, so I told her they were Dutch and Greek, which is abstractly true depending on your views regarding nationhood and immigration and, in the European's eye, cancel out to an inoffensive average. 'Hm...' she said, 'different temperaments,' and smiled approvingly. By the end of the conversation it was clear that Desdemona believed we were kindred spirits, even if divided by a deep class line. She was wealthy enough that I suspected she was very familiar with feeling this distance from people, and that the wealth was a distantly aristocratic inheritance suggested to me that she was irreversibly inclined towards coldness as a result of inbreeding and epigenetics. I also suspected that in some way she enjoyed the pity she felt for me and that exercising warmth and sympathy qualified as a sort of emotional calisthenics for her. I was a more-than-willing receptacle for this emotional expression. She gave me the job and I accepted, although what it entailed remained unclear.

•

At first there was the agency I'd craved. The staff was international so the work was entirely remote and had been since before the pandemic. This, combined with their erratic schedules and the fact that no one worked for the company full-time—other than Desdemona, allegedly—meant that everyone had bypassed the camaraderie other remote officer workers had developed throughout the pandemic, so no one in the company was necessarily friendly nor inclined to talk more than the requisite amount. The lack of clear structures also meant that no one person was truly aware of what was happening across the entire company, which suited me very well, since my job was to assist across all departments. Everyone thought I was busy working on a project for someone else so would only hesitatingly ask me to help them with anything and would also give me generous deadlines. I'd been told the job would be very creative and would 'suit a writer', but it turned out the only writing I had to do was drafting copy for clients' newsletters and press releases—a type of text that is closer to arithmetic than it is to writing. I found its vacuity practically meditative.

For the first month of the job I would stand in my kitchen at ten in the morning in total silence eating sumptuously buttered slices of toast, staring at a wall, just thinking. It felt like everything I'd hoped for and more.

Then Desdemona returned to London after a stint in Paris and wrote to me saying it might be nice if I joined her the next day in her flat in Chelsea. I wasn't sure what this entailed and it certainly hadn't been mentioned as a possibility in the interview or in the month since and, more importantly, I resented the impact this would have on my toast and cogitation schedule. But I simply replied saying that sounded delightful and signed off with 'À demain', which I thought she might enjoy.

Her flat was near mine so I cycled the short journey over the river the next morning. When I arrived at her front door with my bike helmet dangling from the crook of my elbow she found it truly hysterical and, once she'd composed herself, said I really was an 'interesting creature'.

I was surprised by the décor of the flat, which didn't consist of what I'd expected (framed pencil drawings by major twentieth century artists) but Man Ray-like photography and various reflective pieces of furniture. It was, I was astonished to think, nouveau riche. I wondered briefly if the PR company wasn't a vanity project after all; perhaps Desdemona actually *needed* to work.

It transpired that I'd been invited over because she wanted me to run a series of errands for her, including doing her groceries. I was a little surprised because this seemed outside my developing understanding of my strange job, but I wanted to show myself as capable and enthusiastic, so I said of course, I'd be happy to do that, but I needed to send a draft of a press release to the person running the luxury car account first, if she didn't mind. Desdemona waved her hand and said that could wait, but her food couldn't. So I did her errands and when I arrived with the groceries I automatically started unpacking them into her fridge and cupboards. I noticed her observing me doing this and instantly realised I'd made a serious mistake. What I had thought was me displaying capability and enthusiasm was me actually showing Desdemona that I would tolerate demeaning tasks amiably. I'd inadvertently given her permission to treat me like a personal assistant. I hated the idea of becoming so closely entangled with one other person—the thought of coming to know her routines, her dry cleaning, her breakfast choices, revolted me. So I placed the rye bread on the kitchen counter in front of the bread bin and left the rest of the groceries in their shopping bags to join her at the dining table with my laptop, and start drafting the stupid press release.

She tutted to herself as she worked and mumbled in English, then sometimes snatched her phone and had an intense phone call with a client in French. At one point she told me I must help myself to any food or drinks I wanted and gestured to the kitchen and said, 'You know where everything is...'

After some time she seemed to reach a lull and lowered her laptop screen, leaned back and looked at me. She asked what I was working on and I reminded her about the press release, which seemed to perk her up. She asked to see it and before I could answer she rose from her seat and leant over me, closer than I like anyone to be, and looked at my screen. She began to read the text in a whisper and after the first line she went 'no, no, this won't work' and began dictating to me. I hesitatingly typed her correction and then eventually she took the laptop herself and retyped the whole text, while narrating why my version was wrong. I thought her version sounded much worse and less coherent, but she presented me with it and told me this was exactly how I should write all future press releases. I said 'okay', although I knew the only way to achieve this would be to reach her level of intellect, which seemed an unlikely course of events unless I took up running into walls as a hobby. She returned to her laptop and began tutting again, then looked up at me, as if she'd just had an idea, and said, 'I am surprised...' she gestured to my laptop. 'I thought you were a writer.' It was so deliberately cruel and personal that I had nothing to say. That I had nothing to say surprised even me, but it revealed to me that despite my little grocery rebellion, I knew my place entirely and I did not think I deserved better.

Eventually I shrugged lightly, but she wasn't looking at me anymore.

I finished my minor remaining tasks quietly and when I had nothing left to do I began to ask Desdemona if there was anything I could help her with, but she said 'one moment, I must focus' before I could finish my question. So I sat in silence, my humiliation raging so loudly I felt like I couldn't think.

•

Here is a fact that is real: lying does incur a mental cost, regardless of whether it incurs a moral one. In a 2005 study, it was found that habitual liars have an increased amount of white matter in their dorsolateral, prefrontal and orbitofrontal cortex. These areas of the brain are responsible for, among much else, personality formation and memory. A proposed explanation for the increased white matter is that the construction of a lie forces us to be inventive and use our memory to recall the details of our inventions. The demonstrated impact on our personality centre is what led Ariely to suggest that we are permanently weighing how a lie impacts our self-perception. This weight diminishes the more you lie, apparently. You can get into the habit of it easily enough until the weight is insignificant, and then the only cost you may encounter is guilt.

•

Another common interpretation of the 2005 study is that the increase of white matter may be the cause for lying, rather than the symptom—that this type of activity in the brain might inevitably lead to fabulation, and, incidentally, psychopathy. It is worth noting that the study was conducted on ten voluntary participants from temporary employment agencies in Los Angeles, and that five of the participants were not just habitual liars, but specifically malingerers: people who lie to avoid work. That the circumstances that may cause a person to lie are not considered seems to me an oversight, and the implication that someone who lies to get out of work might also be showing signs of psychopathy is a disquieting, or even laughable, leap. Though I would obviously be disinclined from making this assumption, because the fact is that I started lying to Desdemona in ordinary, embarrassing ways, and relentlessly at that.

It was both easier and harder to lie to her than other people. Because of our social distance I felt like we had less language in common, so I was less able to design sophisticated stories for her, but this also meant that she was less likely to query details in a story—anything she found confusing about something I was telling her she would comfortably ascribe to me being poor. So I claimed my bike had been damaged and started taking the bus to her flat. I knew she hadn't used public transport in years so on the first day I arrived by bus I made a comment about how unreliable it was and she nodded sincerely and talked about how ridiculous it was that tube drivers went on strike so often, to which I made a succession of nondescript noises she interpreted as agreement. But with the seed successfully planted I arrived at Desdemona's between fifteen and twenty minutes late every day and welcomed the minor triumph it represented. Every conversation became an opportunity to lie. One day my period was accompanied by unbearable cramps that turned me grey and faint and Desdemona, horrified, instantly ordered me a taxi. The next day I was recovered but implied to her that this was part of a larger medical problem, that I was 'beginning to suspect endometriosis'. Something about it being gynaecological tapped into a well of feminist sympathy and it bought me a monthly three-day break from her.

Every lie I used to get away from her was ostensibly to buy me time to write and to indulge in my life the ways I wanted to, but a few months into the job I started investing these lies into buying time for my third and final strand of employment: Anna.

•

I knew enough about how the world worked to know that by every logic Anna and I should not have crossed paths—she is a journalist of significant standing in an area of writing I have never wished to belong to and also have no right to. Anna writes serious journalism which demands high ethical standards she strives to meet. She interviews people, she sifts through archives, she reads books on her topic, she doorsteps people, her work is rigorously fact-checked before publication. Anna cares about the truth. Before meeting her I'd read a lot of her work in the same way I watched the Olympics: with admiration and a certainty that I could never do any of that myself.

Three months after I'd started working for Desdemona I was at a friend from university's wedding and an older man named Richard, who'd reached that special age where all well-read men become avuncular, asked what I did for work. I told him I was a writer, of course, and he correctly interpreted this as me saying I was an aspiring writer. He said a friend of his in Los Angeles had a daughter who was a writer. Maybe he could put us in touch and she could give me some tips. He took my email and then the topic became Paddy Leigh Fermor, about whom Richard had a great deal to say and I had a great deal of nodding to give in reply. Encouraged by our literary bonding, he let me know that if he'd been younger he would have tried it on with me. I smiled, which you're supposed to, and said 'maybe I like old men', which you're not. He let himself believe me for a second, then called me a minx and left, titillated, with the promise that he'd 'follow up digitally', which I took to mean I could expect a creepy email, although it easily could have been a promise to finger me.

I often had conversations like this, where someone offered their distant connection's professional advice, and they had two likely conclusions: I never heard from the writer who hadn't consented to giving me unsolicited advice, or I did hear from them and they were something like a tabloid journalist (beneath contempt), a copywriter whose parents only half-understood their job (of no use to me) or someone who wasn't actually a writer but introduced themselves as one (useless, pathetic, forgivable).

When I received an email from Anna with the subject line 'via Richard' I was astonished and forced to resentfully thank God for creepy old men. It was a warm email that said she had no plans to be in London anytime soon, but maybe we could have a call, and that she also wondered if she could ask me a favour. We had the call and I made no effort to conceal that while I admired her work, I had no interest in becoming a journalist. I didn't tell her that my writing ambitions were various from the perspective of language and form, but ultimately simple in the sense that I had lots of opinions, that I liked expressing them, and I wanted to write about myself.

The trouble with writing about yourself is that it creates a record of you, which was obviously not convenient for a person whose life mission was to change this record repeatedly. So I'd found a natural home in writing poetry, where there was a decades-long debate about the distance between the speaker of the poem and the poet herself that I didn't think it was my place to try and resolve. I also liked the endorsement that came from my poetry being published and shortlisted for prizes (though crucially never winning) and from being asked to teach poetry (albeit as a form of art therapy for the disabled and elderly, a kind of teaching that is valuable but has a low barrier for entry). I could downplay the effort that I put into my writing by pretending that I just wrote little scraps that benevolent editors published out of pity, but the truth is that I worked hard and with real ambition and was motivated by what could be called an academic curiosity if you are feeling generous, or nosiness if you are not.

This academic curiosity is also why, around the time that I was having this phone call with Anna, I had developed a dissatisfaction with poetry's ability to be informative and persuasive, so had done a natural pivot into essay writing. About two months after this call with Anna I impulsively started a master's degree in creative non-fiction writing, which I had been told would be perfect for me, and then swiftly discovered was not. Early into the course I realised that I had a tendency to inflate circumstances of my life, to round them too well, and to align their telling with conventional narrative structures. In other words, I was lying, and it made me a bad writer. Instead of confronting this fact, I started to retreat. I began to miss seminars, deadlines. And I resented how this would be interpreted. I hated the idea that my tutors or cohort would think I was a frantic, messy person—the kind of person who can't keep track of her schedule, who is chronically late and disorganised, who needs help from those around her. I was none of those things and I was proud not to be. I maintained my rotation of jobs, I was incredibly frugal and managed to stretch my meagre income to impressive lengths, I socialised, I read books, I remembered everyone's birthdays and sent punctual wishes, I paid for insurance for my phone, I returned online shopping early in the return window, I'd never had an STI, and had only got pregnant once. I wasn't messy.

But during this call to Anna I hadn't yet confronted these disappointing realities, so she found me optimistic. I told her about some of the topics I wrote about and that I'd recently turned to writing essays, although was cautious not to talk about myself too much in case she thought I was needy, or stupid. But she herself asked, generously, to hear more about my interests and my writing. She recommended some books that related to my work and mentioned a news story that she'd heard of recently that seemed relevant. The story was incredibly relevant and I was quietly moved by the serious interest she was showing in me and struck by how effortlessly intelligent she seemed. She comfortably pivoted the conversation to the favour she wanted to ask of me: to take pictures of a London street. I would be paid for my time, she said, and then asked how much seemed right to me. I would have done it for free but I said a sum and she said 'hm, no, I think it should be more' and then suggested double the amount. It was half of what I made in a week of working for Desdemona. That these sums were proximate said more about Desdemona's stinginess than it did Anna's generosity, but I was grateful to Anna nonetheless.

I went to the street floating with a sense of real purpose. Anna had explained that the significance of this street was that it connected two pubs, and that two subjects in a forthcoming article had been drinking in these separate pubs for years. Despite the proximity, these two subjects had never met. It was a detail she was intrigued by and she said that she doubted it was significant, but a motif in her article was that 'fate' can be explained by coincidence and coincidence can be explained by imperceptible forms of human rationality. So she wondered if seeing the pubs and the street could explain the coincidence of these two people never meeting, and might serve this motif. I was impressed that her budget extended to substantiating motifs, and when I said as much she laughed, which made me laugh too.

I got to the street at 6pm and discovered that it was barely a street and instead more of an alleyway, which was already promising for my investigation. I took photographs of the alleyway and a two-and-a-half-minute video, but despite its narrowness I couldn't see any obvious reason for the lack of travel between the pubs, so I went to one of them and sat for a drink. I stayed there for an hour, observing, and conceived of some sociological influences (nearest tube stations, football allegiances, quality of lager, how voices carried) that might prevent me from visiting the next pub, then set off to cross the alleyway. Once I emerged it was raining heavily and a number of gutter pipes were spewing rainwater into the alleyway from above, flooding it and entirely smothering my intentions of crossing it. I was ecstatic. I took a video of this too and, to complete my investigation, sprinted through the alleyway and went to the next pub. As I drank there I began drafting notes on my phone, explaining that the rain was the most likely inhibitor of cross-pub travel, but included a number of other things that might explain why these two men would not have met on a dry day either.

When I was home I made a zip folder with all my images and videos and edited my notes. I emailed both to Anna. The email was 600 words long and I kept returning to it to re-read, alternating between being deeply proud and deeply embarrassed by the amount of effort I had invested into this.

She emailed back the next day saying, 'This is amazing!!!! Thank you!!'

When the article came out I immediately control+F searched the word 'pubs'. There were three results. She had mentioned the rain and the flooding.

For a solemn moment I felt my entire body harden—like I became an object that was undeniably real. I heard the smallest sigh as the air diverted around me. In the space of that moment I truly mattered.

The feeling reduced throughout the day—stolen by the slow attrition of speaking to other people, sensing how little material impact I actually had on anything. I could have preserved it if I'd stayed alone. I tried to revisit the feeling by reading the article again and instead found myself feeling moved by the fact that Anna had presented the detail about the rain as if she'd discovered it herself—as if she'd been me. That for a brief moment Anna had tried to be me instead of the other way round offered a rush of something that felt like triumph, something that felt like hatred, but I wasn't sure for whom. The feeling passed before it could be fully named.

•

I didn't hear from Anna for a while. During her silence I rotated through the same emotional performance any rejection triggered: embarrassment over having come on too strong, convincing myself she didn't deserve my effort anyway, shame, again, then listing journalists I thought were far more competent writers than Anna anyway, then thinking of how I could express this list to Anna in a way that was quietly devastating to her but not petty from me, then back to a richer and deeper shame, one where the meat of that feeling had toughened with every other unkind thought I had for myself until it forced me to confront everything I knew was wrong about me. The spiral would conclude there so I could wallow properly.

8.

Four months in, I was still seeing other people alongside Normal Ben—many. This didn't constitute any betrayal to him, to my mind, because I didn't feel he was owed any devotion from me outside of the time I spent with him. But it was clear that he wanted more, and although I liked to give Normal Ben what he wanted, since making a good person happy seemed to offer me some of that goodness too, I didn't want to give up my fun, I didn't want to abandon the exercise in self-invention this variety of people offered me and, crucially, I knew that if I kept seeing him some lie I'd told him would inevitably crumble and take me with it. I obviously couldn't tell him these last two reasons, and he simply did not understand the first. It is difficult to explain a relationship to carnality without granting permission for psychoanalytic interpretation to be projected onto you, and so when I tried to explain it to Normal Ben I could see him hovering over assumptions about my relationship to men, to my body, to being bisexual, to whether or not I had felt attractive as a teenager, but he resisted voicing them, so I never had a chance to dispel them. He clearly couldn't believe that random, casual sex might be more fun than the possibility of commitment and devotion, but he was able to accept that it was my belief, in the way you humour someone who believes in astrology. This too was unvoiced so I could never explicitly accuse him of humouring me, and the silence of the agreement meant that he was allowed to believe that I would change my mind, that I could not correct him, and that he was allowed to want more from me. So the compromise, it seemed, was to continue sleeping with other people, but to see him more often.

Friday nights crept into our rotation, which inevitably invited Saturday morning in, too.

These mornings we'd shift the murk of sleep by giving one another indulgent orgasms in complete silence, our wet mouths open, pressed against skin or each other, thighs grating with the ugly traction of sleep's sweat. I liked his breath in my ear as we lay on our sides and he pressed his way into me, thrusting steadily and robustly. It sounded so sincere and broad, like the deep breath he gave late at night when he moved from consciousness to sleep. I admit that I loved that when he came it sounded like relief.

Then we'd unravel into a new configuration and with each passing Saturday I grew more at ease on his shoulder, gazing out of his window at Camberwell's finest trees, boasting a fresh growth of leaves. Normal Ben had assumed this ease would be enough to change my mind about our situation, and I had assumed that the ease would be enough to please him. This difference of beliefs came to a head on our fourth or fifth Saturday morning.

In the week leading up to this Saturday morning, my father was visiting London, and Normal Ben, who enjoyed stories about my father on account of his unintentional but undeniable eccentricity, had clearly hoped I would invite the two to meet and indicated this by asking, several times, about our plans during the visit. They obviously were not going to meet, so I politely ran through the itinerary and said we'd be very busy, which put a stop to the hints. But this injury was doubled: that same week Normal Ben was reluctantly moving from South to East London and had equally held hopes that I might assist him in the move or, more importantly, attend the 'wake' he had planned for the Saturday night (a pub crawl from Peckham to Camberwell), to mark his departure from London's best quarter. Attending this and meeting his entire social life was also not an option, but I was too cowardly to express this, so I simply said I would think about it but I had a deadline coming up so I might have to spend the weekend working on a poem. The consternation on his face showed that I couldn't have come up with a more insulting excuse.

So the week passed and Normal Ben sent me fewer messages during it (although I'd made an effort to ask how the moving was going) until my father and I emerged from *Madama Butterfly*, an opera about someone dying of patience, and I found Normal Ben, clearly having made note of the itinerary, had sent a message asking 'how was the opera? did you and your dad have a good time'. I was impressed that such a simple message could emanate so much hurt—the absence of a second question mark showed the undiluted depression that until then I thought only a kicked dog could achieve.

As my father joined the long queue of geriatrics waiting for the bathroom, I replied to Normal Ben: 'Opera good, father very pleased, although he did make a point of letting me know that he thinks the libretto is "bilge" several times, but he says that about anything with melodrama. He also let me know that the woman to his right enjoyed the show hugely ("she was going goo goo gaga [sic] about the music") but that when she took a picture of the curtain call he noticed with disappointment that her phone background was a picture of her dog. He didn't explain why this was bad, but he shrugged in a "what are you going to do about it" sort of way.' I thought this degree of detail would represent a kind of peace offering, that it would allow him into my life more. Then, feeling strangely nervous, I followed up the message with 'oh and of course' and sent a picture of my father with his binoculars, which he'd brought from home for the event. And then, thirty seconds later, I sent, 'What are you up to tomorrow night?'

I arrived at his new flat at 11pm the next night, Friday, holding a pomegranate as a housewarming gift. Normal Ben received it by saying 'Wow, thank you, exactly what I needed. What is it? Yeah, okay. A pomegranate. I knew that.' And then looked lost in his kitchen until he decided to put it in the fridge, which was barren but for a half empty jar of pesto and some energy drinks.

As we approached his bedroom I prepared myself to discuss everything that had been unsaid, but then, before we entered, he blocked the door and faced me. 'I have to give you a warning,' he began, and then explained that he hadn't been able to find where he'd packed his bedding, so up until that point he had been using a single bedsheet loaned to him by his flatmate to wrap himself up 'sort of burrito style' and then had been sleeping between the naked mattress and duvet. He acknowledged that this was a 'Neanderthal way of living' and up until the minute I'd arrived he had been tearing through boxes to try and fix the situation, but now I was here and it was too late. 'So I realised my only options were to come clean or to commit seppuku,' he said, 'but, you're not gonna believe this, I can't find where I packed my katana either.' He said he understood if I never wanted to see him again, but if that was my decision, could I help him find the katana before I left?

Although this question seemed to be a vehicle to express a sincere fear of rejection, his peace offering to me was that it was couched in a joke, so that I could either answer the fear or the joke. Frankly I wanted to tell him that I didn't care about the bed, I was just happy to see him, which was a simple emotion and easily expressed, like many of the best ones are. But the cost of this confession still frightened me, and instead I said, 'Threatening to kill yourself if I leave. Textbook emotional abuse, beautifully executed.'

He smiled bashfully. 'Did it work, m'lady? Please say yes. *Pleeeeease* don't make me kill myself.'

I enjoyed looking through the boxes of his things, which were surprisingly neatly packed. We found the box of bedding, which had been left in the kitchen by accident. As he negotiated marrying the duvet to its cover, I slotted the fitted sheet over the mattress. When I bent over the final corner he began pawing at me, stroking my ass and kissing my neck. He was so visibly turned on by this domestic scene that I felt it would be cruel not to get naked. As we fucked he had a small and private smile that transformed into solemn concentration when he came. We slept under the naked duvet.

In the morning, I lay on his shoulder and gazed at the new view from his window, which was punctuated by the minarets of one of east London's mosques. He started talking about the wake, which would start that evening at the Nag's Head on Rye Lane, and before he could remind me that I would be welcome to join I pointed at the mosque and asked if he could hear the call to prayer from here.

'I know I said I was a lapsed Catholic but I didn't say I'd converted,' he said. 'But yes, I can hear the song. I actually think… no, I can't tell you. You'll laugh.'

I swore that I wouldn't. He called me a liar. I begged him to tell me. He resisted, resisted, relented.

'Well. Okay. In the three days since I've moved, every time I've gone to the corner shop the guy's been praying, so I've just had to stand there with my can of Coke for a few minutes while he prays because I think it would be rude to leave—like he might think I'm leaving because he's praying, like I'm offended or something—so I just stand there for a bit, pretending to read a Pringles tube or something, looking baffled by the starch content, and then when he's done he gets up and acts like nothing's happened, which I guess is accurate, and I just pay for my Coke and we say cheers and all that and I leave and—I'm not finished, don't interrupt me, there's more—I wondered if maybe the guy secretly hates me and he's actually pretending to pray each time I go in because he's hoping it'll make me fuck off, and each time I don't he's possibly slightly, against his own will, disappointed that I'm not racist. But I've realised that it's probably the other, more obvious, option.'

'I don't think there is an obvious alternative,' I said.

'It's that every time I hear the call to prayer I want a can of Coke.'

I laughed a lot, not really because I found it funny, but more in recognition of the effort of telling it, and the fact that it was clearly a joke he'd practised on others before. Normal Ben tried to conceal how pleased with himself he was.

'Now I'm not saying that Allah is calling for me to have a Coke,' he continued. 'Maybe it's just that my cravings run on a prayer timetable. Maybe all cravings do. The other option is that it's just coincidence, but I can't believe in that.'

I told him I had to leave to teach retirees how to write poetry, which was actually true, and got halfway dressed before we ended up having sex again. It was efficient—missionary, I didn't even take my bra and T-shirt off and I didn't finish. He told me he owed me one. At his front door I deftly avoided his attempts to undo my shoelaces with his short, undexterous toes and then he asked what

I was thinking about the wake. Could he count on me to be both in attendance and mourning?

I hesitated. For a moment I considered how ridiculous it was that these minor details and mechanisms were dictating so much of our pleasure. It seemed detrimental for no reason other than following social convention that was, ultimately—I thought, indignantly, and not entirely convincingly—patriarchal, and possessive. An after-effect of women being little more than chattel for centuries. The option to express this indignation presented itself, and I knew it would be a slimy and manipulative move, but it felt like the only option I had left.

He spoke before I could, mercifully.

'This is a really boring thing to say, but,' he rolled his eyes and stretched, resting his hands against the doorframe, where he strummed his fingers against the wood. The action replayed across the muscles of his arms, his excellent arms, like the strings in a piano. He postponed speaking even further by yawning.

'Jesus. Spit it out. You want me to come, I get it.'

'No. No, only if you want to. I guess what I want to say is that I want you to want to come. And that, kind of soon, this thing will be painful for me. I guess I feel like I only have half of your attention. And you should probably know this about me, but I want all of it.'

He said the ball was in my court.

'Also, anyway, you have to come back to tell me what to do with this so-called pomegranate.'

'I think—probably—you eat it.'

'What makes you think I've ever bought or used a pomegranate before? Do you think I'm some kind of king? A sultan? My fruit skills are very low. I can just about peel a banana. Give me a satsuma and I'm fucked. A pomegranate? Do you hate me?'

As I said 'that's just so not true, I bet during your beautiful verdant Surrey childhood your mother épluched fresh mangoes, passion fruits and other exotic fruits and then dropped perfectly ripe morsels into your little eager mouth every single night,' he said 'here we go again', 'what is *éplooshed*', 'speak English, woman', 'you are bigoted against the English, bigoted against Surrey, bigoted against mothers,' then, 'and my mother never put anything into my "little mouth", so jot that down'.

With that done, he told me to think about what he'd said. He tucked my hair behind my ear and kissed me gently, sexlessly. It felt good.

•

It goes without saying that he deserved better. You should know I know that.

•

I've been on the other side of this.

My ex-boyfriend Isaac was the worst liar I've ever known. He was undeniably beautiful and charismatic and those features earned him a lot of kindness from others, but he was also one of those unfortunate people who are clever enough to know that they are not as clever as they wish they were, and this mix of ambition and shame had curdled in him. I am also one of those people, so I know the pain of it well.

I can sense another liar in a room like there's been a change of atmosphere and when I first met Isaac it was like the weather had turned; he was the centre in a gaggle of people and leading conversation by making references to artists, philosophers or economic policies in a way that I thought was suspiciously shallow and a familiar conversational sleight of hand. I was astonished that others were falling for it, but I am generally invested in keeping people gullible, so I never said anything. His naked want for attention and the subtle insecurity it stemmed from was magnetic, so I listened to him devotedly and he slowly sank into the pleasure of my attention. We became inseparable and formed a self-sustaining ecosystem—he needed me to listen and I felt incredibly important by listening. I saw through his stories about various betrayals and injuries from friends, family, lovers where his culpability was always diminished and dismissed with a fake acknowledgement like 'I know I'm fucked up' and 'I know what I did was wrong but she should have talked to me about it first'. But nodding along and swallowing the stories despite this was a profound form of communion, and a profound form of dishonesty. I minimised my deceit by repeating his stories to others, to his friends, to mine, to legitimise his account, and I told these stories better than he ever did. I wasn't naive; I knew it would end badly and that I'd have to get out before it did.

The only lies I told him were that his paintings were good and that I didn't want to be a subject of one because I was shy. Any other lies I told him were simple detritus—excuses for being late, books I'd read, that I like radishes. He was so occupied with his own inventions there seemed very little space for mine, which was a brief relief, and for the period that I loved him I slept better than I had in years. It was clear to me that his parents had needed him to love them as best as he could, and I wondered if that might have been when he first learned how to lie.

I did eventually grow bored—of his lack of interest in me, that he clearly thought I wasn't as clever as him, and in the role I'd been playing. I began to withdraw from him as tenderly as I could, and he punished me for it with such catastrophic force that the memory of it sometimes spasms through me like a slipped disc.

Every time I think about Isaac and what he did to me my assessment of the cruelty changes—the outcome seemed so inevitable that I can only sometimes think of myself as a victim. Often I think I deserved it.

9.

On some Tuesday afternoon, about a month after the pub story, Anna messaged me on WhatsApp to ask me if I could record and send her a voice note of an audio file in the British Library archive which she needed to listen to 'almost immediately'. She apologised profusely for the time pressure. I was leaving Desdemona's when I received this and without any hesitation I cancelled my evening plans to get the recording to Anna as close to immediately as possible. I replayed all my conversations with Desdemona from that day in case I needed to extract something into a lie to justify taking the next day off for the purpose of this mission. This turned out not to be necessary—I got the recording within two hours. Anna was very grateful for how quickly I'd managed this and I was forced to recognise that my feelings of abandonment had been irrational and tried to forget how I'd compared her to other journalists—they had very different ambitions, I told myself, and couldn't be fairly compared.

Anna began to pop up with requests along these lines every couple of months, some that required research which I undertook diligently, but the majority being simple logistical things that I knew she only asked me to do because of my location and flexibility. She maintained a warmth and friendliness in all of these exchanges, sent me things she thought related to my own writing, and put me in touch with other journalists who had similar requests. She was the one who'd suggested the master's degree, which she said seemed like it was made for me. When I was accepted onto the course she wrote saying 'O.M.G. YES YES YES! NOT SURPRISED THO' because, despite her many substantial assets, she was still American.

The Saturday I left Normal Ben's with his challenge I'd resolved to ignore him, and I did. For several weeks. This took real fortitude, but I felt there were a number of reasons it was essential that I physically suppress my desire to see him, chief among them being the fear of any lies being discovered, but also a general malaise around the idea of being witnessed and recorded by one person long-term, with its loss of self-determination and reinvention, and the fact that inevitably, at some point, we would grow bored of keeping the record of each other's lives, or lose faith in each other's ability to do so. I am ashamed to say there was also some glimmer of that old-fashioned and laughable conviction that I should 'focus on my work', and that Normal Ben's presence would somehow detract from it, since relationships and this process of being spectated had the tendency to make time sluggish. I regret to say that my irrationality was immediately rewarded when the train that rushed me away from Normal Ben's new flat passed through an underground pocket of phone signal that was strong enough to deliver a message from Anna. She was asking if I had the availability in the next two months to do some work for her that may take two weeks, possibly longer, and would require some more research than I had done for her in the past. She warned that it might be intense. She could explain more details on the phone.

I felt that Anna had a stronger grasp on the world than I did. She seemed to belong to and know how to navigate it with an ease that I desperately wanted but couldn't understand fully enough to emulate. She extracted truthful information from people as well as institutions and she synthesised it with a profound knowledge about her topic in a way that was undeniably and astonishingly insightful. She had real impact. People changed their minds about important topics after reading Anna's articles, and everything she wrote about was true. Anna truly and completely mattered. I thought working for her would make me matter too.

I emailed back within minutes to say I'd have to move a few things around, by which I meant lying to Desdemona even more, but I would be happy to do it, absolutely.

•

It was three weeks into me ignoring Normal Ben. He'd shown real courage in the face of being stood up at his own wake—all he'd sent that Saturday was a message saying 'there couldn't be a better place to be dying to see somebody' and then a meme of a taxidermied fox that was sitting patiently and looked clinically depressed. Two days later he sent a screenshot of the Google search 'can boys eat pomigranite' and then a week later a single, solitary question mark. Then nothing.

I don't have a lot of friends, but I have a small intricate network of people, none of whom it would be acceptable for me to write about in any real detail. We gather and bear witness to each other's lives like a Greek chorus. We narrate to one another, then we disassemble every story, every relationship romantic or otherwise, and examine the axes of power present in them, we analyse who owes whom care, where the responsibility lies, how our gender, class, race and neurodivergence manifest, we align our beliefs across social media and what we read at university, the latest article that everyone is discussing, we talk about sex with indulgent and gratuitous detail, we talk about our parents like we understand them, we use therapy speak, we make fun of therapy speak, we distil our lives down to fable-like significance where every passing encounter is representative of every larger inequality we have been moulded in, where what happens to us represents what happens to everyone, almost all of us have been shaped by sexism and this fact is such a given we find it almost embarrassing to mention when we have been treated like women, even though many of us aren't, we know each other's pains, each other's triggers, we tell each other when we are owed better, we end stories with 'it's not that deep' and then sincerely reply that it is that deep, we take each other's stories at face value, we never challenge each other, we cry with one another, we are patient, loving, in a way that could be considered enabling, we forgive each other instantly, in a way that is enabling, we repeat stories and sometimes they end differently, we know to believe one another, even when we have reason to doubt.

The Chorus wants what is best for me.

The Chorus tells me to return to Normal Ben.

•

All I wanted was control. It was undeniable that my lowest point was when I sat at Desdemona's dining table as she took my laptop and read my emails back to me, letting me know what parts made me sound stupid. I marvelled at how much of my life this woman already owned, and the low price I was willing to sell it for, and often thought it would be easier to murder her than it would be to tell her to stop speaking to me like that; the psychological threshold for bludgeoning her to death seemed so much lower than that for standing up for myself. Temptingly low. It also seemed like the most viable option because, for all our early bonding over languages, we actually seemed to belong to such separate worlds there was literally no way to successfully communicate—her face and emotional expression were totally opaque to me. She would laugh at things that weren't funny, frown when she was speaking to her friends on the phone, especially when the conversation sounded pleasant, and never smiled at strangers. She also often asked me why I looked so upset, before she'd even successfully upset me, and would get annoyed if I said I wasn't upset. We were both products of the punitive French education system—whose pedagogy seemed to rely entirely on humiliation—but where it had taught me to distrust and hate all authority figures, it had taught her that power is, by definition, cruel. I wanted to quit, obviously I did, but I was convinced I couldn't get any other job, so I had no choice but to tolerate her, and because my hatred had no possible outlet, the only way to tolerate her was by returning to the familiar pattern of my school years: to entirely surrender any concept of myself as a person who deserved dignity or kindness and to imagine that I was a barely human. It helped me understand how she saw me. To achieve this it felt like I needed to dislocate parts of my psyche and I always found that in the moments where this snap was successful and I crossed into a space of placid serenity, my mind would then begin to drift to images of flesh, of spitting, twisting, pulling, gasping. Then I felt my control ooze in.

I wore the same outfit on all my first dates and got undressed the same way each time. I'd stopped having second dates. In strangers' bedrooms I would point at their decor and laugh, I would pick up whatever book was nearest to their pillow and read aloud from a random page as if they were a fucking idiot for enjoying whatever it was, I'd ask them how much money they made and make them feel ashamed for answering or not answering, I'd ask them if they thought they were important, I'd tell them a life is valued by how much it would be mourned, I'd tell them about the first time I was sexually assaulted, I'd ask them about the best sex of their life, I'd lick, nibble, suck, squeeze, pinch, tug, grip, hurt, spit as they told me, I'd let them turn themselves on, I'd let them struggle with my jumpsuit, I'd tell them to let me take charge, I'd make them touch themselves while I undressed, I'd tell them no one knew how to undress me, I'd tell them the name of the last person I'd fucked, I'd describe their body, I'd say how much it turned me on, I'd grip, tug, lick, ask them to beg, I'd let them fight back, I'd take the rutting, up against the wall, on the bed, over the desk, the sofa, the chair, I'd let them pull my hair, I'd say harder, harder, I'd say just like that, I'd turn them over, I'd make them describe the feeling, I'd use my nails, I'd try to leave a mark, I'd let the feeling grow, tell them they were good, let it fill the room like a gas, let them to breathe it in, make them, I'd choke, I'd press, I'd whisper, I'd let them quiver, whimper, beg, I'd say good, good, let their eyes roll, just like that, yes, that, let them finish, wet, anywhere, let them pulsate, throb, wet, the body clutching yes, yes, yes, to softness, let them pant, I'd think about how the Facial Action Coding System doesn't have a cum face, I'd let them kiss, let them thank, let them tug, let them try to reciprocate, let them tease, let them thrust, let them thrust, let them thrust, I'd try to let the feeling in, I'd find the seam, sense the split, eyes shut and grasping for the placid serenity, the twisting, the pulling, the standing in the garden in my favourite dress, the feeling like a river running through me, the garden, the garden, the stop, the room forming around me. The ugly posters, the stupid books, the idiot doing their best between my legs. The telling them to stop, the putting my clothes back on and saying I'd had fun, the fast exit, the cold of midnight. The shivering as I pulled out my phone. The knowing this is what he wanted. The texting Normal Ben. The simple punctuation of 'I miss you'. His instant reply.

The standing in his kitchen. Him asking if this is what I wanted. Tipping my head back. Saying yes, yes. This. Kissing my open mouth. Twisting my skirt into his fist. Making me beg. This. Yes, this, yes, I want this. Pulling me down the sofa, pressing me open, pressing in the sign of benediction, the slow, the ebb, the grip, the egging me on, the eyes on me, the build, the tight, the gasp, the feeling rushing in, the gripping his hair, the pressing against him, the begging, the body hanging from the rafters, the crook of his finger, the body's dark blue lips, the feeling, the feeling, the surrender, the cataclysm of its entrance, its entrance, its entrance, the blank slate. The feeling afterwards.

•

He said I should know that he loves me.

I believed him, I believed I deserved it, I believed I loved him back. I said it, laughing, crying, naked, and on the way home I watched a person leap into the Thames and envied their weightless, peaceful form until they struck the water with all that inevitable force.

PART TWO

1.

Although the specifics vary in each country, it is almost universal that the police are held to be agents of truth, whose primary purpose, when a crime occurs, is to extract the truth of the event, determine who is culpable, and deliver the responsible person to the courts. The courts will then determine whether the police were correct and dole out the punishment if they were. This design rests on a few given facts: that the punishment of the law is significant enough that a perpetrator will conceal their action to avoid the consequences, and that, therefore, the police will have to root out the liar in the pursuit of justice. The police achieve this through a combination of examining material evidence and talking to people. An alarming number of crimes are solved through talking to people. An alarming number of convictions rest on testimony instead of material evidence.

American policing pioneered many of the techniques used by police forces around the world. Since the mid-century, American police have used an interrogation method named the Reid technique, developed by John E. Reid in 1955, while he investigated a murder case in Nebraska. In the course of his investigation he used a series of psychological tricks to successfully extract a confession from the murdered woman's husband, Darrel Parker. Had Parker not confessed, they would never have been able to convict him, and it was thanks to Reid's methods that they'd received the confession. So the Reid technique was born.

The Reid technique understands the criminal mind. It understands that people have a preservation instinct and will not be induced into self-incrimination unless the police use sophisticated psychological tactics. Their most useful tactic is this: they lie to you. This is not a shady and unofficial practice, it is the official practice that is in their rulebook: each of the five editions of *Criminal Interrogation and Confessions*, the manual for the Reid technique, state that police interrogation, by necessity, requires deception. Since the guilty person will not be inclined to volunteer a confession, the investigator is obliged to use these tactics that the author of the fifth edition does admit 'could well be classified as "unethical"', but, it goes on, 'investigators must deal with criminal suspects on a somewhat lower moral plane'.

Reid and Fred E. Inbau, a lawyer and criminologist, collaboratively wrote the manuals for this method of interrogation. The method outlives them both. Reid developed the technique in the 50s, founded John E. Reid & Associates, Inc, and then died in the 80s, after which Inbau continued the research and issuing of further instruction manuals until he too died, in a traffic accident, while developing the fourth edition. Methods can easily outlive their inventors though; John E. Reid & Associates,

Inc has trained so many law enforcement agencies—from police to the FBI, CIA, secret services, and private security companies—that the method survives comfortably. It is a method that serves the lie detectors well, there is no reason for it to die.

The threshold for being dragged to this 'lower moral plane' is being considered a suspect, and whether or not you are a suspect is at the police's discretion. You should know that they can tell—they can see it on your face.

•

Anna told me the solicitors' office were expecting me at 8am. The solicitors' office were entirely surprised by my arrival at 8am and the office manager, a young woman named Olivia, asked me to take a seat on a plastic chair in a damp room as she spent about 40 minutes working out what to do with me. Eventually it was worked out that I was indeed meant to be visiting and after a further period of waiting on my chair Olivia invited me into a different, and much smaller, damp room. The whole building had the municipal feel more than half the buildings in the UK have, and this second room was especially devoid of personality—like its design was based entirely on meeting fire safety regulations and the council's construction standards at the time it was built. It never ceases to amaze me that every building that matches this description—and is therefore the consequence of a thousand intricate decisions made by various regulatory bodies—still fails to prevent damp and mould, as if this country being wet is a remarkable occurrence that could not possibly be planned for. Olivia apologised profusely for having made me wait then said if I needed anything, either today or over the next few days I was supposed to be here, she would do her best to help. The visible sincerity she said this with did nothing to diminish the implication that any request I had would likely be impossible to fulfil. She gave a nervous wave and then left, shutting the door gingerly. The room was plunged into a wet silence, like every thought I had needed to crawl out of my head to wade through the suspended moisture.

There was a desk and one chair. Occupying the desk and half of the available floor were six large cardboard boxes. Each had 'Crawley' written across them in thick pen and some were labelled 'defence', 'prosecution' and 'interviews', alongside sequences of numbers that meant nothing to me. I cleared the table by moving the boxes, shifting each to the floor, until I placed the one labelled 'interviews' on the chair beside to me. I unboxed it and was faced with a stack of manila folders. I removed the first one and slid out its contents onto the desk. It was an inch-thick sheaf that I held up and tapped against the table, patting the sides until the pages' edges aligned. I lowered the sheaf onto the table and barely acknowledged the writing on the front page as I took out my phone to open a scanner app. I felt each of these gestures emerge from me with the ease and familiarity of swimming, casting invisible ripples in the air. But the truth was that I had no idea what I was doing, nor why I was doing it. At the entrance Olivia had made me fill out a visitor's form and where it asked for the purpose of my visit I'd written 'journalism' although this felt far from accurate.

I'd waited for Anna to call me the night before and fifteen minutes after we'd arranged to speak she texted to say that something had come up, so she couldn't call. She sent a screenshot of an address (the solicitors' office) and told me they were expecting me at 8am—all I needed to do was scan the documents they would present me with. I asked if there was anything else I needed to know, and did she need me to read the documents too and give a summary of them, or anything along those lines? She said it would be great if I could, but really the priority should be to scan them all—I should only worry about reading if I had enough spare time. I wanted to ask if something had changed and if I was still going to have to do research, or anything more intelligent than scanning, but I worried that doing this would seem like I was ungrateful for her trust in me, so I didn't say anything. But I was unhappy. I felt that Anna was deliberately withholding something from me and on the 7:10am train that morning I had begun to feel a strange anger. The second I'd glimpsed the six boxes in that room I'd known I wouldn't have time to do anything other than scan and the anger became impossible to ignore. It seemed obvious that Anna had known from the start that all she needed me to do was this stupid task, but had dangled the promise of me doing more serious research for her so I would be inclined to change my schedule and prioritise her. I resented that she'd felt the need to lie to me and I resented how hurt it made me. I am embarrassed to admit that it also filled me with a consuming desire to prove her wrong for thinking so little of me, and it felt like the only way to do this was to become indispensable, to give her information she wouldn't otherwise have, to think faster and sharper than she could, so I put my phone aside and began to read the document in front of me.

•

At this point it is important to note that Anna has not consented to me writing about her. Her name is not Anna and, to avoid anything identifying, I have fictionalised many of the details surrounding her. Everything I tell you about Anna is concealed beneath a veil of fiction, but I am truthfully representing the dynamic of our relationship, and the type of work I did for her. The specifics are the only things I will ever lie to you about.

Anna's article based on the work I did in that solicitor's office was not published, but out of respect for its subjects, I have done my best to anonymise the material that relates to them. I have done this in a way that does not compromise on what I perceive to be significant truths of this investigation; I hope you will understand and not think worse of me for this. In any case, the violence that occurred between these two people is so common it could apply to anyone. I could reinvent the story in a million different configurations and the outcome would almost always be the same.

•

As with every crime, there is more than one story. Lily's story is that she was raped; Michael's is that she wasn't.

•

Included in the boxes, among pages and pages of text under the solicitors' letterhead, were: a statement from the university where Michael is a lecturer and Lily was a student, a letter from Michael to the university's disciplinary committee, a letter from Michael to the investigative committee, sixty-five pages of scans of Lily's phone contents including messages, notes and emails, fifteen pages of scans from her diary, reports from a physical exam (Lily's), reports from a psychological assessment (Lily's), medical records (Lily's), medication history (Lily's), statements from two of Michael's colleagues addressed to the disciplinary committee, one statement from a student of Michael's also to the disciplinary committee, a handwritten letter from Lily's mother addressed to whom it may concern, a typed letter from Lily's flatmate addressed to the disciplinary committee, a letter from the investigative committee to the disciplinary committee, a statement from the disciplinary committee addressed to Michael, a letter from the investigative committee addressed to the police, two police interviews with Lily, two police interviews with Michael, a photograph of Michael, taken by the police. He looked like I'd expected.

•

The Reid technique has three stages: firstly, the police acquire information through physical evidence, then they undertake a series of interviews with the people in connection with the crime (witnesses, relatives or other people with relevant connections to the event), and then, once they have reason to suspect someone, they undertake an interrogation.

Interviews and interrogations are distinct. The interview is non-accusatory—a more casual process where the conversation approaches free-flow; the investigator can ask their questions but permit the interviewee to direct to other topics. The design of this is three-fold: the interviewer gains more information, incriminating or otherwise, develops a rapport with the interviewee, and, crucially, can study their behavioural responses: 'posture, eye contact, facial expression, and word choice, as well as response delivery may each reveal signs of truthfulness or deception'.

The police can tell when you are lying thanks to two features: they are trained in detecting non-verbal indicators of deceit, and they also know what the truth looks like. When they are interviewing a suspect, they will tell, from their stillness, from their fidgeting, from their hesitation, from their assertiveness, from their direct eye contact, from their avoidant gaze, from their crossed arms, from their open ones, from their slow breathing, from their hyperventilating, from the fact that they come from the sort of people that do things like this, that the suspect is guilty. They will know. Then they can launch the interrogation, where accusation enters.

It is crucial that the interrogator reveal no weakness—the suspect must believe they have been found out. According to the manual, the following statement will not be effective: 'Joe, I think you may have had something to do with starting this fire'. Instead, the interrogator must say: 'Joe, there is absolutely no doubt that you were the person who started this fire'. If Joe did not start the fire, it will be obvious in his defence and the interrogator will be able to detect his truth in the telling.

You should know that the purpose of the Reid technique is not to find the guilty party, but to extract a confession. To achieve this, although it may surprise you, the detective displays empathy: they tell the suspect that anyone in their circumstances would have done the same thing, and then they begin to invent stories to explain why the suspect did what they did. It is vital that the detective prevents the suspect from denying the accusation during the course of the interrogation, so instead the detective gives the suspect options for why they committed the crime, one deplorable, and one justifiable, and then presents them to the suspect. The manual gives many examples, like, 'Did you plan on doing this for months in advance or did it just happen on the spur of the moment?' or 'Did you steal that money to buy drugs and booze or did you need it to take care of your family?' An opportunity for denial is not presented. You may think that you would be unlikely to fall for this, but you might be inclined to confess after the detective has lied to you and told you he has all the evidence he needs to convict you. After a detective has told you that there is no doubt, Joe, that you started this fire and he has your fingerprints all over that tin of lighter fluid, he has witnesses who saw you there, he knows you did it, but did you do it for a deplorable reason or a forgivable one, and this story goes two ways, he's seen it time and time again, he's seen what happens to people who do things for deplorable reasons, and he's seen what happens to troubled souls who do bad things for simple and forgivable reasons, you may say you did it, you may say you did it for a good reason.

There is no way to know exactly how many false confessions the Reid technique has secured but it is likely very, very many, and the count started in 1955, when Darrel Parker, Reid's first victim, was coerced into confessing to a crime he didn't commit. His wife had been killed by a stranger. In 1970 Parker was released from custody, in 1991 he was formally pardoned, in 2011 the state of Nebraska gave him half a million dollars in compensation. Parker, then eighty years old, announced, 'Now, I can die in peace'.

•

If one wanted to extend John E. Reid the hand of forgiveness, one would only have to shrug and say that his methods were downstream of far less sophisticated methods of lie detection. Chewing on rice, hot pokers on tongues, and so on. Suspects have suffered worse than sitting in rooms where they are given two options. And Reid was not alone—law-enforcement across the world, certainly the English-speaking world, has participated in similarly poor practices. Both the American and British police have been faced with a number of scandals around false convictions, but in the UK, unlike the US, policing changed.

Shortly before the turn of the millennium, the British police adopted the PEACE model for investigative interviewing, a method that had been developed by a committee of detectives and psychologists in 1992. The model dispenses with interrogations and instead commits itself entirely to lengthy, detailed interviews, where the purpose is purely fact-finding. The investigator, either a Police Constable or a Detective Constable, is transparent about this. Crucially, the method does not allow for deception. In fact, the only instance where the PEACE method is deceitful is in its own name, which allegedly stands for Preparation and Planning; Engage and Explain; Account, Clarify and Challenge; Closure; Evaluation, but we must admit that PPEEACCCE is less memorable.

The method can afford to lose the focus on coercion and deceit because the PEACE method is not interested in gaining a confession—it is interested in gaining information. The process of a PEACE-style interview is questions, and then questions, and then questions. The secondary purpose of this method of interviewing is exhausting its subject, although this aspect of the method is not made known to its subject.

•

I started with the transcripts of Michael's interviews. The first one began with the PC explaining a lengthy series of bureaucratic details that spans several pages: he said the interview is being recorded, introduced himself, asked Michael to confirm his name and date of birth, and then said 'I'll just state the facts' and the facts he stated are the date and time, the police station the interview was happening in, and that Michael was under caution, meaning that he did not *have* to answer any of the questions but it may harm his defence if something he later relied on in court was not mentioned during this interview. Then the PC asked Michael's solicitor to introduce himself, for the tape, which Michael's solicitor did, although addressed to Michael. It is the solicitor whose offices I am sitting in. Then the PC emphasised that Michael was under no obligation to reply—no one was forcing him. After each of these details, the PC asked 'Do you understand?' and Michael alternated between saying 'yes', 'I do', 'yeah', 'okay', and 'of course'. The PC advised him that although the interview was being filmed, the primary record was the tape recording, so Michael was asked to reply audibly each time and avoid non-verbal answers. Michael said 'Okay, yeah, okay'. Then the PC explained that he was also going to take some notes on paper, but that Michael should try not to be distracted by that. Then the transcript reports the PC saying 'Now, we have reason to suspect that you have committed a crime. We are investigating this crime so we will be speaking to everyone we can, we will be investigating all the evidence available to us, and this is your opportunity to help with this investigation and tell me what you know about the event on 3 March 2019 that led to this investigation and what you think I should know about it. I will be asking you specific details about that night but I will also be asking you about yourself. I will ask you about your relationship with Miss Lily Kilgore, and we can discuss other topics if you like. I hope you are going to speak to me and answer my questions. Before we start, I need you to know that I cannot lie to you. I can't tell you that I know something if I don't know it. I can't lie to get you to talk to me. Do you understand?' and Michael said 'yes, yes, understood' and the PC replied 'I hope you are going to tell me the truth. I will be checking everything you say, okay? To make sure it is true,' and Michael said 'okay'. Then the interview was ready to begin.

•

Thought has a kind of weight. That white matter clustering around the brain. The basis of the PEACE method is to induce cognitive overload in a suspect, to trip them up. The PEACE method is only interested in verbal signs of lying. Technically, the interview could be conducted with the lights off. The lying suspect will be remembering what truly happened and will be striving to align their deceit with the truth—will be sustaining real mental effort to achieve this. The lying suspect will be tired out—what they say will begin to collide with the real world—the truth will overrule. This method works best when there is real, solid evidence surrounding a story. The method works less when the only evidence is memory, when the evidence is what is said happened. When the only evidence is memory, cognitive overload destroys the evidence.

•

Anna texted to ask me how it was going. I hadn't scanned a single thing. The truth was that after an initial assessment of the interviews I'd felt a powerful revulsion that I'd suppressed by subjecting myself to a series of minor physical discomforts like pinching the soft of my wrists or pressing the heel of my hand into my eyes, then sat on the floor with my open laptop reading about police interrogation methods, ignoring the paperwork. I was surprised to hear from her since it was 5am where she was and resented the immediate stomach-drop it brought on. I'd expected to encounter the feeling later in the day. I texted back saying 'slow start—problem with the office this morning and took a long time to get it sorted. Scanning now, will send you what I've got through at the end of the day.' I hovered over asking for more information—why I was even here. She reacted to the message with a thumbs up. I put my phone away.

I went to get a meal deal and sat by the canal to eat it. It was an unseasonably humid day; every smell was intensified, the odour molecules suspended in the sluggish air, unmistakably rotting. In the water below, a blanket of algae hugged the outline of a corpse, face down and almost static apart from the slightest drift. Its hair was slicked flat and through the parting the scalp shone bright like a white and bloodless wound.

I tugged a pilfered packet of chewing gum out from my sleeve and chewed as I checked my emails, not that I was expecting anything. There was one from the university reminding me that I was expected to rejoin the course in one term's time. I immediately decided to pretend I'd never seen it. It was hard to ignore a mounting restless and violent melancholy. I wanted to hurt something. Instead, I sifted through my spam folder until I found a comically vibrant email about penis enlargement. I forwarded it to Normal Ben's work email, which he'd asked me not to use after the last time, with the note 'this was erroneously sent to my junk folder. I thought it would be of use to you, so I am forwarding it on' and signed off with my kindest regards and one exclamation mark. He replied a few minutes later from his personal email, which he'd forwarded the spam to, thanking me for passing this on as he was extremely interested in these services, but advised that I forward similar communication to this email address instead. He signed off, 'Yours hornily, Normal Ben'.

A second later he texted me saying 'you're going to get me fired. when can I see you?' I answered 'tonight' instantly, a little surprised by how much I wanted to see him, and how comforting the thought of him was. He promised to come over after attending a pub quiz then asked how the scanning was going. I sent him the crazy eyes emoji, the cartwheel emoji, the dolphin emoji. He replied with a thumbs up and the top hat emoji. He'd understood me perfectly.

On the way back to the solicitor's office I picked up an expensive iced coffee for Olivia and asked her when the latest I could leave the office was, because I had a lot left to get through.

•

I ploughed through as much scanning as I could in a few hours so that Anna wouldn't suspect I'd wasted the day sitting on the floor researching interrogation techniques.

At 6pm Olivia knocked on the door and told me she was clocking off and because I was a visitor I had to leave too. She was very apologetic about this and said she'd stayed as late as she could to give me extra time, but had to leave now because she had plans with her boyfriend. I was taken aback by this unexpected act of kindness and felt like the only way to express real gratitude was to interrogate her about her life, her boyfriend, whether she was vegetarian and what her evening plans were. She told me she'd grown up in the area, had studied Criminology, was still deciding if she wanted to pursue that professional avenue, was indeed vegetarian, and was going to the cinema with her boyfriend but she couldn't remember the name of the film they were seeing. She then asked me if I was a journalist and with no hesitation I said I was. I thought it would incline her towards helping me more. I was idly conscious of the fact that Anna gaining access to these files was likely a result of indicating to the solicitors that she was writing a story in Michael's favour—cooperation has to be acquired somehow, and the cost-benefit analysis of this lie had an obvious outcome, I thought.

When I was on the train home Normal Ben called me to ask how my day had gone, which I found a perverse instinct both because I hated phone calls and because he was going to see me later that night anyway and could hear about my day then. I told him as much.

'Please try and be a normal person for twenty minutes,' he said. 'And I'll probably be pissed tonight so this might be our only chance for a back and forth today. Tonight might only be back, no forth.'

So I spent thirty minutes telling him about body language analysis, interrogation methods, about Olivia not remembering the film she was going to see that evening and how baffling I found it that she was going to volunteer nearly three hours of her time to an unknown film chosen by her boyfriend. 'I also found out a weird thing,' I said. 'Did you know that lapsed Catholics have one of the highest rates of kleptomania?'

'What? Really?'

'No, not at all. But did you believe me for a moment? Because that shows a part of you could believe it to be true. A part of you might think you have potential to be criminal… If it could be true then it might be true.'

He said that wasn't how the world works. Then he asked me why Anna needed the research, he thought I'd just be scanning.

'Well,' I hesitated. Normal Ben held a low opinion of Anna. I attributed this to jealousy, because my respect and admiration for her was so blatant. I'd tried to show off to him once by showing him the few sentences across her articles that could be entirely credited to something I'd researched for her and he, cooly, concealing the embers of envy, said that just sounded like she was stealing my ideas. So I couldn't tell him the truth, which was that I wanted to impress her by giving her my ideas. Instead I said, 'It's a long story. Anyway, I don't tell you how to do your job.'

'That's cause you don't understand my job.'

He wasn't wrong.

That night I continued my research and began writing it into notes for Anna, until Normal Ben turned up at my door incandescently drunk. He slurred 'Keep those away from me,' pointing to my toes, and then, during the several minutes it took for him to successfully remove his coat and obsessively tightly laced shoelaces, he told me about his night at the pub quiz which, it transpired, was only pretending to be a normal pub quiz but was in fact a ruse designed to ambush men with what was still, in fact, a pub quiz, but one revolving around raising awareness for men's mental health. He explained that the first question of the pub quiz was 'Lads, how are you doing?' and then, once that had been met with a confused silence, the second question was 'No, really. *How are you doing?*' and the quiz master explained that this was an opportunity for men to actually share their feelings with one another, instead of hiding behind banter.

'You see, it wasn't your average pub quiz,' Normal Ben said with a notable lack of mirth. 'It was an excuse for men to get together, share some pints and actually talk to each other.'

'But you already do that all the time. It's literally all you do.' I actually wasn't sure what Normal Ben and his friends, nor any men, really, spoke about when they were alone, but I did know that they drank and spoke to each other all the time.

'I know!'

'And? *How was everyone doing*?'

'You won't believe this,' he said, the left foot triumphantly emerging from his shoe, 'but everyone was doing alright.'

'But did they really, *really* mean it?' I asked.

'Now that's a different question. Who's to say!'

'You know how you could tell if they really meant it?'

He glanced at me and despite the glassiness of his eyes there was the very sincere fear that I would start talking about Paul Ekman. 'Please, no,' he said. 'No more Eccles. No more. Please.'

Then I gently guided him up the stairs as he told me that the problem with being sincere about your feelings was that it was actually very boring, 'And you know what isn't really boring? Drinking lots of pints.' Halfway up the stairs he feigned profound exhaustion and pretended he might collapse on me so I had to support his weight, even though if he did fall it would probably have proved fatal for me, a detail I knew he enjoyed and wanted me to voice. Once we summited the stairs and entered my room I said, 'It's funny how if you fell on me it would probably be fatal,' and he instantly snatched me up, threw me on the bed and collapsed his entire weight on me.

'Is it?' he asked. 'Are you dead yet?' and began tormenting me with a flurry of benign physical assaults to make me yelp and thrash. The rest of what he said wasn't entirely audible over my shrieks but it definitely included a lot of mocking requests to tell him more about policing methods. When I landed a jab in his ribs he groaned, grabbed my wrists and pinned them above my head then trapped my legs with his thighs until I was entirely immobilised beneath him, panting like a cornered rabbit. He looked down at me smugly.

'I win.'

He rolled off me and filled the room with a contented sigh. He mumbled, 'I fucking love you. I'm so happy I can say that. I love you. You're my favourite. I love you,' and gripped my hand like it belonged to him. He kissed the back of it, as he always did. I pictured everything he knew about me, everything I thought he should know about me, as a cluster of threads clutched in his palm, holding this version of me fast. I saw the events of my life rendered smooth, chronological and consequential. I imagined if he let go I would disintegrate completely. I thought of the many things I was frightened of in my life already and how, in that moment, the image of his loosening hand was the worst of them all. I thought of the solicitor's office. The PC telling Michael he could stop the interview if he needed and that the door was not locked.

'I'm so proud of myself,' Normal Ben said. 'So proud I drank enough to fix my men's mental health.'

•

I rarely think of my first year of living in the UK because I find the memories humiliating—the naively looking around and understanding so little, standing in an office asking where I was supposed to be, being moved from place to place and being asked if I understood and saying yes although I wasn't sure I did, feeling like I was a child again; knowing that my father was going through the same process in a council building somewhere, with scans of his children's British passports and scans of his foreign ones. The surprise when submitting one form somewhere seemed to ripple through all these invisible branches and a light would switch on in a room I had not known existed. The sense that I could do something wrong and switch off every light by accident—the paranoia, impossible to resist, of feeling watched. The sense that I had to understand the mechanisms of this place to live here. The sense that a person could be bad at living if they don't understand the rules and don't know how to play by them. I thought of it a lot the week I was at the solicitors' office, though.

•

I went to the solicitors' office for a total of five days that hold no distinction in my mind—when I caught the train each morning I did not feel like I was travelling a physical distance but simply returning to the same static moment in a small damp room where time had no effect. Each morning the room welcomed me into its thick silence with a mess of papers cascading across every surface. The fire door closed behind me automatically, heavy and airtight. I moved the papers mechanically, scanning swiftly, allowing a mental haze to descend as I sifted over events that had already happened, whose conclusion had already been found, whose characters I would never speak to or come to know anything more about. It felt like I was Anna's phantom limb, disturbing a hideous event that was as real as any object, but that I was no person, no thing.

•

Lily gave two police interviews.

•

I will not tell you exactly what happened on 3 March 2019. It would be a terrible thing if Lily were to pick up this book one day and then land upon yet another person repeating this story through an understanding that is not hers. In anonymising the material, it is my hope that this act of kindness never finds its beneficiary. I hope that Lily will not recognise herself in this at all. In any case, I repeat, what happened that night could have happened to anyone.

•

What I can tell you about Lily's two interviews is that during the first one, the PC's questions seemed to be roving through a simple recounting of the night, of the relationship, of Lily's life generally but that small phrases like 'for the record' or 'to be specific, you mean he used his ___ to ___' float to the surface. What I can tell you is that in the pages and pages of scans from Lily's diary, from her phone messages to her friends, to Michael, language like 'fucked' and 'cunt' and 'licking cum' is used and in the police interview she uses phrases like 'penetrated', like 'private area', and then, timidly, after saying 'I don't know how to...', 'ejaculated'. I can tell you that there is the distinct feeling that Lily is trying to get something right—that after a couple of instances of the PC asking for clarity Lily takes on this task herself, she pre-empts the question, that she repeats herself several times, that she narrows in on specific details, that she describes the dress she was wearing that night carefully and how difficult it was to remove, that she cries when the PC asked if she had had anything to drink that night, taken any drugs, that I am only assuming she cries because the transcript has the PC offering her a tissue and asking if she wants to take a break, that Lily says 'I don't want to get in trouble', that the PC says they just need all the facts, that they needed to know what happened, that Lily admits to having taken drugs, that she says 'I'm sorry' three times when she can't remember what time this all happened. I can tell you that I think the story is credible, but what I think is irrelevant.

•

Michael's interviews came after Lily's first one and his language is different. He answers what is asked and nothing more. The solicitor intervenes, just letting Michael know he doesn't need to answer. Michael says things like 'she initiated conversation outside of our tutorials' and 'I understood this to mean' and 'this developed into a physical relationship'. There is the same effect of someone doing their best to get something right, but Michael's rendition is better honed than Lily's and has an element of being rehearsed. This is not necessarily incriminating—it is the result of a good solicitor imparting to his client that he is speaking on the record. Innocent people can sound rehearsed. The PC asks Michael to define what 'a physical relationship' means and Michael does, it means sex, and then the solicitor says nothing more needs to be explained. The PC also asks questions about Michael's life and his work, then about his other relationships, which Michael declines to answer, and what his relationships with his students are like and Michael says 'professional'. When it gets to 3 March the language becomes 'we began to have sex', 'I understood her to be saying' and the PC asks about alcohol and drugs and Michael says Lily had asked him to get drugs and the PC asks how Lily asked and Michael says 'verbally' and the PC asks if Michael can say what she said and he says he 'can't recall, sorry' and the PC says 'you can't recall' and Michael says 'sorry' and then, unprompted, Michael says that Lily had told him about doing drugs before so he wasn't surprised by the request, he thought she did them a lot. Lily had given the impression of being a mature woman with a great deal of experience so Michael was confident she was fully and consensually participating in their relationship. The PC asks a lot of questions about 3 March and Michael says it was normal and then says things like 'she initiated sex' and 'I understood her to be asking me to' and 'I believe we had an ordinary night' and he is consistent in these answers. A letter from July 2019 shows that Michael is charged with rape, although I don't know what evidence leads the police to do this—these procedures are opaque.

•

Most of the English-speaking world operates under common law—the law of precedent. Every ruling either repeats what has come before or brings new rule into law. There is a principle of fairness within this, the notion that how others have been treated is how you will be treated, but there is also a frightening implication to it: how others have been treated is how you will be treated. A significant precedent is the right to remain silent and it is understood that silence remains someone's best defence.

•

We are ambiently aware of what is believable—of what people think is true, whether or not it is real. When the only evidence for a crime is memory, the victim begins to anticipate the investigation, being interviewed, having to narrate. Sometimes they begin to behave like a perfect victim before a crime has even occurred. They confront cruelty with placidity, they face violence with calm, to guarantee that they will be believed as a victim.

•

Some night that week, unbolting Normal Ben's belt buckle, making him hard, telling him to keep still, fucking him, the usual motions, fucking him, hard, nails in his arm, his chest, fucking him, the thought that I am being fucked, that I have been fucked before, the tightening grip, the head rush, the field of vision, the dimming, the finishing, the saying I love him, or whatever, of course I do, the deep breath, the closing my eyes to find sleep, that simpler place, him asking what I'm thinking about, answering honestly, saying Isaac, enduring the quiet that follows, finding sleep, that better place.

•

Sixty-eight years after Reid first used his new method, American police are so familiar with practicing it that they deploy it by default. American women who report sexual assaults have increasingly begun to be subjected to lengthy Reid-style interviews where officers prod at their stories and, satisfied that the details aren't robust, charge the women with making a false report and wasting police time. The police know what a true story looks like—they know what happens to people, so they can put themselves in your shoes, they can see your perspective, they can ask: did you lie for attention or was it because you were embarrassed?

•

You should know that the geographic and practical distance between the UK police and US police is less significant than you think; a layperson is largely ignorant about the law and acquires knowledge of it the same way they come to learn all social behaviour—they pay attention, they watch TV, they imitate, they read headlines, they come to believe certain things are true, whether or not they are, sometimes simply because they feel they should be true, sometimes because they fear they are.

•

Some lunchtime that week, at the canal with my rotting companion, watching videos on my phone of a body language expert warning 'ladies' that a man who doesn't dimple his chin sympathetically is certain to be a narcissist—comments from women asking what else they should look out for—links to the expert's course.

•

Two people enter a room, an event happens, an injury happens, an event trapped in time happens, two people have an event happen to them, one person has an event done to them, two people are trapped in an event in a room, two people exit a room, two people have an event happening to them, two people have an event that happened happening to them, two people narrate what event happened, two people narrate the event to the police, two people narrate to the police again, two people narrate on the record what happened, two people narrate who they are, two people narrate what they did, two people narrate who did what, to whom and how, the police record it, the police record an event, the police record an event again, the record of an event is assembled, the record is assembled into a story, the record could be assembled in any direction, the record is assembled into this story, this story is reassembled by the defence and presented to a jury, this story is reassembled by the prosecution and presented to a jury, this story is decided upon, this story is in a selection of boxes and printed on paper, this story is a cascade of papers in any order I want them, the event is the story, the story is what I make of it, the story is what I believe could have happened, my story is true, my story is what I believe happened, it is what I believe.

•

Lily's second interview is different. This interview is only a day after her previous one and what has happened between these two interviews is up to our imagination, as is what happened between Lily and Michael. She shows less apprehension and instead anticipates the PC's questions—at times she answers questions that haven't been asked. She says 'I'm not a heavy drinker' when the PC asks how the rest of her university life is going and 'I'm the first in my family to go to uni'. Where the PC asks why she kept her relationship with Michael a secret, the document, which is formatted like the script of a play and has the PC's questions in lowercase and everyone's replies in block caps, shows I GAVE YOU MY PHONE, AND MY DIARY, I HAVE TOLD YOU EVERYTHING ALREADY, I'M NOT MAKING THIS UP and you should know that I found myself wondering what her face looked like as she said this, despite it all, because the PC's response suggests she wasn't angry, and in Lily's diary, the one she's citing as evidence, the pages that have been scanned contained violent erotic poems and you should know that I am ashamed of myself for this but my first thought is that the lyric *I* is not a documentary *I* and that I don't believe a creative exercise should be read as representative of its creator, I don't believe that the poems are evidence of anything other than her creative curiosity about abjection, that you should know based on everything I have learned about Lily in these boxes—Lily the First Class English Literature student—means I suspect she'd agree with me, you should know I think she is simply doing her best to provide evidence because she thinks no one is listening and you should know the PC says 'This is just for the record' and Lily says 'I know.'

•

In the 2000s, Paul Ekman co-ran the 'Wizards Project'. This project intended to study how good people were at detecting lies and, after a series of tests both on people working in law-enforcement and on ordinary laypeople, the results were—as Ekman's often are—definitive: people are terrible at detecting lies. On average, we have a 50% chance at detecting a lie—it's essentially guessing. The good news for Ekman is that this result is correct and has been substantiated by similar studies. The bad news is that Ekman's subsequent result, that training will improve someone's ability to detect a lie, is wrong. Saul Kassin, a psychologist with a focus on justice and jury psychology, has devoted years to the study of coercive policing methods and in 2006 wrote a critical appraisal of modern police interrogations, covering all forms of non-verbal lie detection training. The conclusion of Kassin's research directly opposed Ekman's: '[S]pecial training in deception detection may lead investigators to make pre-judgments of guilt, with high confidence, that are biased and frequently in error.' By now you will be familiar with the lethal combination that confidence and inaccuracy represent. You should know that this knowledge has had very little impact on modern policing.

•

A train every evening taking me home, a train every morning returning me to the room, the damp, the smell, like rotting, like decomposing, the scanning, the indifferently warped scans, pages and pages, the body wilting in the canal, the feeling in my stomach, Normal Ben sending encouragement every day from his desk, his happy life that I belong to, the fact that Anna will be using this for something, the fact that I don't know what, the fact that it's my hand, the fact that it's me in the room, that there is a shadow in some scans from me getting too close, the fact that when I Google Michael I can't find anything later than 2019, the fact that when I Google Lily I find nothing at all, the fact that I want to find the trial, the fact that I want a verdict to tell me what happened or what I should believe, that I truly won't feel this story is finished until there is a trial, the fact that on the fifth day I scan the final sheet and realise there is no resolution, the fact that there is no trial, the fact that I look through the scans, the boxes, the papers, to see what I have missed, the fact that I did miss a letter from July 2020 saying the investigation is now ceasing, the fact that it is ceasing because of a lack of 'witness participation', the fact that Lily withdrew from the case, the fact that I have to decide why she did, the fact that Lily and Michael are ignorant of my passage through their lives, the fact that they have passed through mine, the fact that I have to come to my own conclusion, the fact that my conclusion will be shaped by my bias and the fact that I might not be able to control this. The body, disintegrating into parts, drifts and spins like a parting wave as I walk past to my final train home.

•

The lower moral plane. Saul Kassin saying 'When you lie to people about reality, when you misrepresent reality, you can produce profound changes in people's visual perceptions, beliefs, autobiographical memories.' Wondering what plane I'm on.

•

Stopped at a traffic light, from the top deck of the bus I watched someone bleed out onto the pavement, a puncture at their jugular vomiting blood in convulsions, the dark puddle growing senselessly large, and I thought about how I'd told Normal Ben that I was in the school choir, that I was bullied when I was nine, that I broke my arm the first time I wore rollerblades, that I loved my cat, that the accident was reasonably traumatising, that we were friendly with our neighbours, that my ballet teacher fat-shamed me, that it took me much longer than normal to learn how to swim, that by the time she was drinking prescribed meal supplements we all began to accept she might be dying, that I got to see her corpse, that I fainted at the funeral, that I don't have much memory of the years after that, that based on its impact on the course of my life my mother's death was the most important thing that has ever happened to me, that because of its centrality I never allow myself to wish she hadn't died, that I failed half my GCSEs, that we moved to this country carrying one suitcase each, that I've read *Wuthering Heights*, that I have strong thoughts about *Wuthering Heights*, that I'd never seen snow like that before, that we didn't own a fridge for several months, that my first kiss was good, that I had no fear about leaving home, that I preferred living alone actually, that I was surprised by how much I excelled academically, that the sex I was having was obviously sophomoric but informed my tastes nonetheless, that I cheated on my university boyfriend and was surprised by how much it broke his heart, that I thought he wouldn't care, that he was the one who decided it was best we stop speaking to each other, that I didn't move on quickly, that it was only after this that I began to feel like an adult, that I'd moved to Clapham reluctantly, that I'd pitied Isaac from the start, that I felt there was no possibility of returning to the version of me that had existed before Isaac, that I hadn't spoken to Isaac in nearly two years, that I still occasionally felt remorse about the cheating, that I wasn't fucking many people, that I once slept with a man to charge my phone, that the abortion wasn't a big deal and I thought of it as a rite of passage, that I didn't call him Normal Ben in real life that's just what he was saved as on my phone, that I got ready very quickly because I don't really wear makeup, that I wasn't dressing to impress him, that I wasn't going out of my way and I would have done it for anyone, that I found the body, that I found the body and had never told anyone this before, that I really meant it, of course I did, I meant it and was so happy I could finally say it too, and then I thought about how not all of these facts were true.

The body drained its colour onto the pavement and people walked through the stain without even noticing, tracking the blood behind them like a red shadow.

It was a matter of time before one of these facts would be upturned—a simple matter of time before Normal Ben learned to hate me, and I couldn't let it happen on his terms. I had to confess to everything. I had to tell him the entire truth in reverse chronological order so I could unstitch what he'd come to believe about me until we were detached. Then we'd never speak again—this was the only solution.

As I approached the pub he saw me through the window and waved, a smile emerging from him so naturally it felt like I deserved it. I had the choice between smiling back or acknowledging the window above the pub which framed the still outline of a man hanging from his dressing gown belt. I smiled. I grinned.

•

Later that night as he went down on me I did my best to grip his hair and gasp, but I couldn't drown out the sound of a woman screaming for help from the street. I searched for the seam in my mind but her voice grew louder and louder until, finally and brutally, she died. I endured the silence left behind until I sensed her body growing cold, then I had to beg him to stop, please, stop stop stop. He withdrew and asked if I was okay but I was mute with tears and the start of horrible, rattling breaths. He adopted a practicality I'd never seen him display before. He pulled me upright and told me I was having a panic attack, which I suppose I was. As he instructed me on how to breathe and whispered that I was okay, I was okay, it was okay, he gripped my hands and maintained steady, focused eye-contact. It occurred to me that I'd never heard him speak without that veil of irony. His face looked older and I was startled to see something that looked like true pain play across it.

Once the panic had abated he went to get me a glass of water. When he returned he stood by the bed and then asked if it was okay for him to touch me and the apprehension in his voice alarmed me. I took his hand and pulled him in so I could rest my head on his shoulder. He took long, steady breaths, but seemed intent on keeping as still as possible.

In almost every conversation in my life I visualise the possible outcomes of speaking—I predict the consequences and feel the myriad outcomes overlay into a dense, heavy future. In this moment I couldn't see anything. The translucent Normal Ben had become solid and inscrutable. I knew that in that moment the only thing I could do was admit that I was a liar, that that was why I'd had a panic attack. But I couldn't sense what would happen if I did. So in the absence of prediction, I stayed quiet.

It felt like a long time had passed and I thought he'd fallen asleep, but then he broke the silence with the same practical and sincere voice. 'Did I do something wrong?'

I said that he hadn't and pawed at him childishly, desperately.

His breathing slowed but I sensed that he had something else he wanted to say.

'Do you think…' he started, then paused. 'Do you think the case and the research is… bringing things up?' I ran cold. He continued, disjointedly, as if it hurt: 'I guess I assumed that, when you said… I assumed that the situation with Isaac was…' he steadied himself. 'Has the case been triggering?'

You should know that I truly did not know what to say.

I sensed the body in the street like a phantom limb. An involuntary dry sob moved through me—a rattling gasp.

He held me tight and whispered a rotation of comforting phrases and told me we didn't have to talk about it. It was okay, he said. He understood.

One of the easiest ways to beat a lie detector is to say nothing at all. If you refuse to speak, it is practically impossible to lie. You can remain silent—you have a right to.

I cried, fear seeping out of me and pooling on Normal Ben's chest. He wiped my face with his thumb and said it was okay and pressed his chin into the crown of my head. He said he understood. I listened to his honest, unflinching heartbeat. The steady systolic. He really meant it.

I felt the earth rotating. I felt its axis shift. I said nothing.

2.

THE POLYGRAPH DOESN'T WORK.

You should know that this statement is not technically true. The polygraph machine does work and is still used regularly as an interrogation tool that serves the purpose law enforcement wants it to, which is to intimidate. In this sense it works, but it does not actually work, at least not in the way we believe it to.

Five or six sensors are attached to the subject. These sensors include, typically, two pneumographs (hollow, spiral rubber tubes that are wrapped around the chest and abdomen) which measure breathing, a blood-pressure cuff measuring, obviously, blood pressure, and typically two galvanometers, which are small metal plates clamped on the subject's fingers that measure the skin's ability to conduct electricity, which increases with perspiration. These sensors are connected to the machine, which in the case of analogue polygraphs is then connected to three slender needles that spindle out jagged lines on a rolling and seemingly endless sheet of paper, each delivered line corresponding to the subject's breathing, blood pressure and perspiration. This image will be familiar because it is used in visual culture so often, but the truth is that polygraph machines have gone the way of most things and are now digital; new machines operate in exactly the same way as the old ones, but the needles and paper have been replaced by a fairly normal-looking laptop, although the nostalgic may be satisfied to know that the standard-issue laptop does look suitably archaic. Polygraph machines are devices, not people, and are therefore incapable of lying, just as they are incapable of detecting lies. The art of lie detection is fully contained within the polygraph examiner, the person who attaches the sensors to the subject, asks them questions and then, as the subject answers, reads the graph lines carefully, interpreting from them whether the subject is being truthful or not. The vast majority of polygraph examiners are independent contractors who are employed to administer polygraph tests in circumstances like job interviews, family disputes and corporate theft. It is only a minority of them who work directly for law enforcement. Several summaries I read about the profession warn that this role requires undertaking a training course, accreditation from established agencies, and is best suited to those who can drive and own a car because they will have to transport their own equipment to each job. Incidentally, this is incredibly similar to what it takes to be a professional clown, but entry to clowning schools is more competitive. The people who become polygraph examiners do tend to have a background in law enforcement, and I can only assume that they discovered a proclivity or talent for interrogation in the line of duty and that this passion developed into the pursuit of further study. Becoming a polygraph examiner requires approximately 400 hours of training undertaken in no less than ten weeks but no more than seventeen, and of these 400 hours, forty are devoted to studying psychology and physiology, thirty-two involve studying how to compose testing questions, forty on how to analyse the resultant data, and four hours are committed to studying the ethics of this entire practice. Of the remaining 284 hours, the vast majority are dedicated to practicing polygraph tests, so most of the training is actually simply doing.

You should also know that the term isn't technically 'polygraph examiner'. In 1992, Dr. William J. Yankee, a former detective turned polygraph examiner turned academic (his doctorate was in education, specifically focused on the training and education of polygraph examiners), introduced the term 'forensic psychophysiologist' as a more appropriate alternative to 'polygraph examiner', as it captured the scope of the medical and social expertise the examiner brings to their profession. Evidently a pioneer in the science of polygraphy, the American Polygraph Association honoured Yankee with the creation of the William J. Yankee Memorial Scholarship in 1999, a scholarship that funds one promising individual's training in polygraphy each year. This being said, despite it being their technical title, it is frankly very rare to come across the term 'forensic psychophysiologist' in any of the literature written about polygraphy, including in texts written by the American Polygraph Association itself. I actually only told you about this term because I thought you should know that they think of themselves as scientists.

The machine does not detect lying, it detects fear, and polygraph examiners know this. Evy Pompouras, a former polygraph examiner and Secret Service special agent, now memoirist, is not a polygrapher of any particular note but she is one of the many who now seem to make a living by going on podcasts to give tips on how to detect liars. During one of these podcast appearances, she offers a useful analogy: if you are driving down the road, on the edge of, or perhaps slightly above, the speed limit and you drive past a police car, you will feel fearful and slow down. As Poumpouras says: '[Y]ou feel that emotional change in your body. You didn't tell your body to do it, your body just did it for you because it's preparing you.' The same happens when you lie, she says—the 'body and the mind understand it to be a threat.' Of course, Poumpouras's example of a speeding driver is unintentionally revealing: you see the police, you feel fear. You will likely feel this fear whether you are lying or not, especially if you think the police are able to read your mind using a machine. I think of Lily, telling the PC that she has handed over her phone, her diary. I imagine her heart rate as she spoke, and what the fear of not being believed must feel like. Whether it is different from other shades of fear, like the fear of being caught in a lie.

The polygraph machine as we know it was developed slowly in the first half of the twentieth century by a few obsessive American men, though the only one of these men I need you to know about is William Moulton Marston, who principally developed a lie detection machine that measured systolic blood-pressure because he hoped its invention would prevent innocent people from being convicted for crimes they did not commit. Good intentions in this field are so uncommon that they merit suspicion, but I find Marston's devotion to justice surprisingly credible since, nearly twenty years after designing his polygraph, he made a surprising move into the arts and created Wonder Woman, a comic book character whose devotion to justice is facilitated by her golden lasso, which, when bound around someone, prevents them from lying. His research and prototype machine were foundational in the development of improved polygraphs over the following decades, and in the late 1930s the FBI purchased one of the polygraph machine prototypes and mainly used it to screen applicants to the Bureau, a practice they maintain to this day along with most American law enforcement and government agencies. This remains the primary use of polygraph testing: as a screening step in a hiring process.

Given its American roots, it makes sense that the legality, use and ethics of polygraph testing are largely litigated by the precedents set by the American legal system. The first attempt to use evidence gathered by a polygraph in court was in the US in 1923, in the case of Frye vs United States, and the subsequent rejection of it became a landmark ruling known as the Frye Standard, which effectively prohibited the use of 'experimental technologies' as expert testimonies. Since this ruling, eighteen US states have ruled that polygraph testing can be used as court evidence, provided both the prosecution and the defence agree to its use. Should the prosecution be inclined to reject its use, they will likely weigh this decision against the fact that, on average, people perceive the refusal to take a polygraph as an indication of guilt.

Curiously, in the case of Frye vs United States, the person advocating the use of the polygraph test was the defendant, Frye himself, not the prosecution. James Alfonso Frye had been arrested under suspicion of robbery, and during his interrogation for this crime he confessed to an unrelated murder that had occurred over a year earlier. At the time of Frye's arrest, exactly sixteen months after this murder had occurred, the victim's family were offering a substantial reward for the capture of the murderer, and Frye claimed that the detective interrogating him had persuaded him to confess to the murder, with the promise of splitting the reward money between them. I am not sure if he ever received his promised half of the bounty, but he did receive a life sentence. Frye declared he was innocent and said he'd been coerced into this confession, and convinced at least one person of this: William Moulton Marston, who sought to use his recently developed polygraph machine to prove it. Frye undertook a polygraph test and Marston then testified that the machine confirmed it: Frye was innocent, the confession had been false. It was with this evidence that Frye appealed his conviction and it was the court's rejection of this appeal that established the landmark Frye Standard. Frye's conviction of guilt was maintained, as was the sentence for life in prison.

It is worth noting that Frye was black, and although I cannot even begin to suggest whether he was or wasn't guilty, I can say it is hard to imagine any circumstances where any evidence he offered the courts would have allowed his word to overpower that of the white detective who allegedly bribed him to confess.

At the heart of every pseudo-scientific method of lie detection lies a surprising tragedy: the lost potential for provable innocence. I cannot resent Marston for his wish to invent a machine that would offer something good; who among us wouldn't want the same? He is certainly not the first person to have had their invention corrupted by the world it belongs to, and he has learned this lesson more than most—the scale of its corruption is almost beyond belief, and yet, somehow, I manage to believe it.

•

In the morning I was quiet and Normal Ben was normal. I watched him go through his morning routine which always ended with him applying his face cream so aggressively I wondered if his face owed him money. Violently moisturised, he then looked at me and smiled, sat on the bed next to me like I was a convalescent and tucked my hair behind my ear.

His gaze seemed expectant, like he wanted my face to demonstrate the new need, the hurt, he thought he'd discovered in me, but instead it felt like a solid mask. I turned into my pillow so he couldn't look at me.

'Hey, hey.' He pulled my arm and dragged me into an embrace.

I asked him if he still loved me. He couldn't say no, you're not allowed to say no to that question. So he laughed and said yes, so far he was reasonably certain he'd be capable of loving me under most circumstances.

It was a relief that he was the liar for once.

'What if I turned out to be a murderer?'

'Yeah, I'd probably manage. But only if you killed someone who deserves it. Like a paedophile or something.'

'Paedophiles have rights too you know, they deserve a fair trial.'

'Okay,' he released me and turned to knot his shoelaces six or seven times, making sure I was out of reach. 'Sounds to me like you're back to your normal self.'

Before leaving he tucked my hair again and held me tightly. 'It's all good,' he said, 'you're good, be happy.'

•

I walked to Sainsbury's to steal some chewing gum and buy some expensive ham.

Up until that point, everything Normal Ben believed about me was something I'd wanted him to believe, and now he seemed to believe something I hadn't even told him. From the way he tucked my hair, his pitying, steady tone, it was clear he had a certainty about something that not even I was certain about.

The junction at the end of my road was blocked by the wreckage of a car. There was glass everywhere and a cataclysm of metal, plastic, tread marks—the stench of burnt rubber. The car hollowed like a metal skeleton.

I couldn't see the driver anywhere. I rerouted to go to Co-op instead.

I had let Normal Ben believe it though. I hadn't said a thing.

I found the driver down the road, smeared across the asphalt.

•

After giving a coerced confession the suspect tends to recant very quickly. Out of the interrogation room, steady on their feet again, they realise how much their perception of the world was warped by a detective lying to them. They come to remind themselves that they haven't done what they are accused of. So they recant—say the confession was acquired under duress.

But it's too late; there is no taking it back. And a jury is more likely to convict if the suspect has confessed, because the logic we all seem to go by is that a person will not admit to something incriminating unless it is true. The resultant philosophy is that you can be taken at your word if you are admitting to your worst, but not in other circumstances, and that once something has been said it cannot be unsaid.

•

The cost-benefit analysis to lying: is the benefit of the lie worth the possibility of its fallout?

•

I intended to confront him about it that night. To tell him that I thought he'd leapt to an assumption that I wasn't sure I agreed with. I expected this would pull at a loose thread and unspool everything else I'd told him and throughout the day, as I typed up my notes for Anna, I also examined the dimensions of every lie I'd told him and prepared every filthy trick it would take to get out of this. I approached it like preparing a case for myself. I nursed some wrath inside of me to deploy and conceal any other emotion he might provoke, wrath at the unfairness of his assumption, his shallow conclusion that every fucked-up slut was a rape victim. I prepared how I would tell him this and still have him love me.

I ate my expensive ham. I thought of telling him the truth instead, not that I was sure what it was. I prepared for his rage, for his sadness, for his disappointment, for his neediness, for his accusations, for his forgiveness. I prepared for it all.

•

You should know that occasionally the small details of our lives, vast as they may be to us, are humbled by coincidence. So that evening, the very moment I'd intended to tell Normal Ben that either I didn't want to speak about this again or that we should speak about it now, we each looked down at our phones and saw a news notification that said the Queen had died, and laughed at this so much, and for so many hours, that it eclipsed everything else since, after all, laughing is why we liked each other.

•

This is how it went: Normal Ben texted me throughout the morning telling me he loved me several times—messages I ignored in favour of writing my notes for Anna and the occasional interval of lying on the floor to eat some ham. Eventually he messaged asking if I was okay and I replied '????' then 'Whatever makes you ask that!!!!' and he deleted his message and sent 'sorry, that was for my other girlfriend' and then asked to come over that evening, straight after work. He wanted to provide the pleasure of his company.

He arrived around twenty past six holding a packet of Haribo and when I politely declined them with a wave he said 'come here, come here, come here,' and then gently, like a golden retriever holds a dead animal, he put me in a headlock and pressed the sweets through my sealed lips. He stroked my hair as I chewed, theatrically slowly, and shushed me like I was a baby. Then he told me it had been a weird day at work—very nervy, something was definitely going on. I asked if maybe they'd discovered an infinite source of energy; a perpetual motion machine and finally, at last, the Department of Energy would save the world. He told me not to joke about that, it wasn't funny because 'that day will come and you'll be too cynical to believe it and it'll be your loss. You'll be the Doubting Thomas.'

I always thought he looked more beautiful when he made religious references and for a second I let his features glow to me, his face so honest and kind. The thought of kissing it. The thought like a minor death. The feeling grew, the feeling passed.

I told him I wanted to talk about last night. His face tensed into all the solemnity I'd come to expect when he thought about my rape that may or may not have happened. And then our phones—a flash. An involuntary glance that we both pretended not to have done until the crucial words 'Queen Elizabeth' and 'died' stood out to us. The immediate quieting sense of a historical moment that neither of us cared about. How small we felt regardless. How happy, how relieved.

•

The thing about laughter is that it wastes time, and that is a very noble pursuit.

•

I am not proud of it, but it is amazing how much can change from simply making up your mind. The outcome of the cost-benefit analysis was that I would do what it took to be loved. I would even risk losing it.

•

I sent Anna the last of the scans and attached a four-thousand-word document on lie detection and policing methods that began by describing the origin of emotions and facial expressions, which I thought could be persuasive if I'd told it well enough. I did not consider re-reading it after I'd hit send.

•

All Normal Ben and I did was talk, everywhere. In pubs. Near the pond. In his car. On the tube over the sound of screaming gears. Everywhere.

In a strange act of impulsivity Normal Ben paid for us to go to Porto for a weekend and he did that English thing of marvelling at how cheap everything was, being astonished by the flavour of tomatoes, or how cold and simply better the beer was, and at one point he made a comment about benefits of the Mediterranean diet and then paused, reddened, and went 'shut up, shut up, shut up' when I simply said 'Atlantic Ocean, babe, not Mediterranean,' but the truth was I was having just as good a time as he was, was grateful to be somewhere else, and also thought the beer was nice and cold and everything impressively cheap.

Later on the beach I read my book as he dug an impressive hole and told me about sediment and then, tired from his digging, he reclined in the sun and announced the Protestant work ethic was to blame for the UK being a miserable shithole. I put my book down.

'Say that again,' I said, and made a rectangular frame with my fingers and held it up to my eye like it was a camera recording him. He said, 'I think England is miserable because of the Prot—' and I went '*Normal Ben* has been on the Mediterranean diet for *less than one day* and already the results are *clear'* in an American accent. He told me to fuck off. 'Also,' I added, 'trust a Catholic to blame Protestants for everything.'

'Yeah, well… sometimes I just wish I could get Martin Luther and…' he mimed beating the shit out of a small man.

I asked him what other secret opinions he held. He told me to go first.

I pretended to think for a moment then I told him that I thought the principal question of our time was whether we can resolve the ways we hurt each other, both structurally and interpersonally, from prisons to racism, sexism, ableism, and whether we have a duty to prevent harm to one another, on any scale. He told me that was wrong, he said it was climate change. I told him those were the same thing.

He told me that he knew it was an embarrassing opinion but he didn't get contemporary art that just had nothing going on—white canvases, big scribbles, that sort of thing. I slipped into that patronising tone that culture people use when they sense an opportunity to educate a philistine and told him that maybe that was the point of it, that looking at these nothing canvases allowed him to see how he made sense of something; that his indifference could be something revealing to him, like, maybe he's not an associative thinker. He said he just wasn't that interested in himself. He wasn't enough of a narcissist to look at a work of art and think about himself.

I told him I thought we were all living in each other's childhoods—that we were all formed so much by our parents, our experiences of growing up, that it was impossible to correct them fully and that everyone was just a walking result of what had happened to them up until the age of about sixteen, and he said that I was wrong, that people changed as adults, he asked me how what I'd said was any different than believing in Darwinism and then he looked at me like he'd got me, which he had. He said, 'Have I got you?' and I said 'You have got me' and then he punched the air and said 'Get that camera out again, bring it back' so I reluctantly formed the rectangle again with my fingers while he flexed at it and then thrashed about like a football player who'd just scored a goal.

We talked everywhere. It felt like what we said mattered less. It felt like there was less Normal Ben had to know about me. It felt like I didn't need to lie to him anymore. It felt like it was just a matter of time until he asked me about something I couldn't prove and then time would be over. But this hadn't happened yet.

In our Airbnb we got excited about the variety of new surfaces to fuck on and sampled most of them in creative configurations until eventually the fun unravelled into honest, hard thrusting, over the bathroom sink, facing the mirror and watching my ordinary face and his with an expression that is hard to describe, it was something like 4E+58, or 17C+26A.

•

On the flight back he gripped my hand as he slept. In the passport queue I tested his patience by jabbing my finger in his bellybutton, his open yawning mouth, and eventually he clamped my hands by my side and recited what a lovely weekend we'd had and then, in the same breath, said that on the plane he'd had a dream about me finding that body in Battersea Park. Wasn't that weird? he asked. It was, I said. It was.

•

In 2009, Fox released a crime drama called *Lie to Me*, where Tim Roth plays an English psychologist with all the trademark hip swings, smirks and lazy enunciation we have come to associate with the arrogant genius TV character. Roth didn't know it, I assume, but this show would have a serious impact on the world. As Cal Lightman, Roth swaggers about corridors and then into police interrogations and tells the police that they're fucking morons and rambles off a bunch of science that they can't keep up with and ultimately concludes, again, that they're morons, they're bad at their jobs and they're missing everything, then he points at a paused screen, showing the recording of their interrogation, where the suspect is grimacing in a particular way and he says that the suspect's raised lip is a classic sign of derision and that *that* is a sign of lying.

In the second scene of the first episode, Lightman gives a lecture to a room full of slightly sceptical law enforcement officers, explaining that emotions are universal to all people—they're instinct, you know. One of the audience members leans over to the other and says 'I hear he went and studied a tribe in the jungle' and then an image of Paul Ekman in Papua New Guinea is shown where his face has been replaced with Tim Roth's.

You should know that Paul Ekman claims he insisted to the producers that the character of Cal Lightman should not resemble him—he wasn't interested in this being about him.

You should know that in 2019, a paper authored by fifty-two academics outlined what I can only describe as an epidemic of pseudoscience about non-verbal communication in the justice system, in policing methods, and, though this is not their own fault, in juries. *Lie to Me* is cited as one of the many roots of this misinformation in juries. A further study on subjects who had watched the show confirmed that they were more likely to detect lies where there were none. It seems necessary to remind you of Saul Kassin's research: the more someone thinks they can spot a liar, the worse they are at it, but the more confident they become.

•

You should know that Ekman is only mentioned in the 2019 report once, among a sea of names who are culpable. But Ekman is the one who found the evidence that turned belief into a fact, so he is the one I care about the most.

•

Something being disproven doesn't mean it stops being used. It is common knowledge that the polygraph doesn't work, and yet it is used all the time outside of the courtroom because it remains a useful tool. The FBI and the CIA allegedly have a habit of using the polygraph to intimidate their own agents and, recently, FBI agents have reported being subjected to polygraph tests in which they are asked whether they respect the Trump-appointed chief of the bureau.

The polygraph's use in British policing also increases steadily, particularly by the Probation Service, who will administer a polygraph test on people convicted of serious sexual offences or terrorism, to judge whether they are at risk of re-offending after release. It is not surprising that people guilty of these crimes are the threshold the polygraph creeps over—when civil liberties are peeled back, legislation is often tested on characters who are reviled. It is therefore not surprising that there are also often idle queries in the UK about whether the polygraph can be introduced into the process of applying for benefits or asylum.

•

The FACS will share a similar fate. It will be further integrated into other lie-detecting technologies which will in turn be discredited when evidence of their faults and false conclusions begins to emerge. These technologies will be condemned and criticised, and they will continue to be used. This is what will happen, because we've seen it happen before.

•

By his own definition, we don't know if Paul Ekman is a liar because we don't know if he intended to deceive. As I wrote my notes for Anna, I watched videos of Ekman being interviewed and I found him charismatic, a natural storyteller who speaks about his wife fondly, jokes about how naturally dexterous his face is, shows off how he can wiggle his eyebrows independently, and how he might be able to credit his career to this skill. As I watched him speak it struck me that I know enough to know I can't tell if he's a liar. As I watched I drafted an email—addressed to an address I found on the Ekman Group website—that began 'Dear Dr Ekman/to whom it may concern' and said in the body that I wondered if he might be available for a brief conversation. I wrote that I worked for the publication Anna was writing for. I thought of my rules—that this might make me worse than a liar, it might make me a fraud. I hit send. The email bounced back thirty seconds later. The intention to deceive was present.

•

Anna's reply came a month after I'd sent the scans. I'd successfully repressed the thought of her in that time and when I saw she'd replied I felt about it like you do about medical results: I didn't want to know what it said and I wanted to read it immediately.

Hiya,

Thank you for the scanning!! I know the travel was inconvenient and I am thankful that you were able to take this on at a short notice. Sorry it took me so long to answer. The deadline got bumped up so I had to file this faster than I've ever filed anything before. Then the piece got killed haha. Typical.

I read through the research you sent but I'm confused. Is this something you are working on? Do you want feedback?

Thanks again!
Anna

I wrote back making polite notes about how I was grateful for the work and to be involved in her process again. The fact was that I was upset with her though. At the time I went through a number of sophisticated rationalisations that concluded with her failing in her role as an employer and mentor, and I wanted to indicate to her that she should involve me more significantly. But the fact was that I had come to see that I'd operated with blind faith in everything she'd asked of me until now and, for the first time, I didn't trust her. Whatever she wanted to do with this case and this story—I didn't trust that it would be good. I had no right to this feeling, but it was there, and there was nothing I could do about it. So the rest of my message said:

As for the research, thank you for reading it! Sorry I wasn't clearer—no feedback is needed, although I appreciate the offer. I only included it with the hope that it could be of use to you. I wasn't sure what the story you were writing was about and in the absence of guidance I had to leap to my own conclusions. I felt passionately that the material should be contextualised within an understanding of the possibility for truth to be misconstrued, misrepresented, or indeed entirely invented then recorded in these environments. I have many doubts about policing methods—which I hope you can agree are well-founded, based on the evidence—and I don't think these documents can allow anyone to develop a real understanding of what happened between Michael and Lily. But it alarms me that this is now the official record of what happened, especially when the process of acquiring this record likely destroyed the chance of any form of justice. There are conventional narratives being projected onto both of them, most of all Lily, and I couldn't in good conscience deliver this material without raising my concerns about all of this.

I'm sad to hear the story was killed though, as I would have loved to read what it was about, and I have no doubt it was excellent. Forgive me for this next request, which I understand is significant, but you may understand why I am making it: in future, I would love if you could share more about your intention behind the work I am being asked to do. I do not want to encroach on your practice at all, but I would also like to have the ability to understand what my efforts are serving, if that makes sense?

And I signed off with my very best wishes.

•

The next day.

Hi,

I am sorry if I gave you a reason to believe that I was going to write about this story in a way that the truth might be "misrepresented". I do understand your request to be given more insight, which I believe I am correct to read as a desire to operate in a way you deem ethical?

You too can understand, I hope, my perspective here. Your email suggests to me that you do not trust me to operate in a way that you approve of, ethically, or to write a story that is, by your standards, truthful. This is surprising. I cannot imagine any of my work so far has led you to this impression.

These are criticisms I take very seriously. You understand in my profession integrity and honesty are paramount, and these values have to be maintained to do what is necessary: ask difficult questions about complicated stories and represent them truthfully, even when that truth is not apparent. I agree with you that conventional narratives, as you put it, are being used in this event. This is what my piece was about, to some extent. I am not saying this to comfort you, but to let you know that I am disappointed you doubted this at all.

You should have received payment, including the cost of transport.

Anna
Sent from my iPhone

•

A follow-up, a moment later.

This is obviously something you are passionate about. You should write about it.

•

I knew I'd never hear from her again.

It took some effort, but I pretended I'd never received the emails.

When I came close to this thought, I'd pause, scratch at my arms or twist my hair around my index finger and pull, hard and long, then I'd find myself returning to normal. I saw a couple of bodies around that time. Fresh—the blood still flowing, an indescribable mangle of flesh, muscles, bones. Nothing notable.

•

A good liar is perceptive and eloquent, they have a quasi-prophetic sense of how their words will operate in the future and they also have an inviolable recollection of everything they've said so far. Good liars know exactly how to perform their normal selves, because there is nothing beneath the performance. You should know that I am a very good liar. It is nothing to be proud of, but I am.

I am not asking for sympathy, because I know I don't deserve it, but you should know it is exhausting to be this way. Around when that feeling lodged in my stomach and I discovered lying, I also acquired a tendency for insomnia that has shown a grim persistence since. It is not, as you might expect, a case of abating rabid guilt each time I try to sleep, but more a reluctance to surrender to sleep and relinquish the perfect solitude of night, when I can finally stop thinking.

•

Scratching my arms, tugging my hair, I pictured myself at five years old, standing in the garden alone, wearing my favourite dress—my parents out of sight. A perfect solitude. Realising I could do anything I wanted. No one was in charge but me. That this would end as soon as I went home, where my parents would love me as best as they could. Feeling a melancholy slip in. Forcing myself to smile.

•

The process of medical diagnosis is essentially an attempt to classify the patient's symptoms in a way that may align with pre-existing conditions which have received successful treatment. Physical conditions are diagnosed in a process akin to a police investigation: a combination of the patient's testimony, physical evidence and test results confirm the condition they suffer from. In the case of most mental disorders, however, the patient's testimony is almost all the diagnostician has to rely on, and through a process of questioning and self-reporting, it is established whether the patient's experience corresponds with an adequate number of the diagnostic criteria to qualify for a diagnosis. In the case of all the mental disorders pathological lying is a symptom of, it is not an essential criterion for diagnosis. That is to say that a patient could be correctly diagnosed with a personality disorder with no need to mention their compulsive inclination towards deceit. In other words, a pathological liar is only caught when they turn themselves in, and that only happens when they've ruined their life, which is a stage I haven't reached yet.

•

Since the night of the panic attack, I felt like I had dug my fingernails into the ground and willed the world to come to a standstill. I felt that I'd been surprisingly successful, but Anna's departure disturbed the equilibrium in a number of ways. The primary impact was the loss of income, and to correct this I reluctantly admitted that I had to commit to Desdemona with full sincerity.

So, shortly after Anna's reply, I spent a weekend willing myself into fortitude, into the clear and honest conviction that I liked Desdemona, I liked the job, and that I would become much better at it, because it was undeniable that I was actually a terrible employee. But this could change, I told myself.

•

When I arrived the next day Desdemona was in a kind of animal mood. As much as her behaviour often made little sense to me, anger is fairly unambiguous, and I had practice in shrinking from its heat. From the moment she'd opened the door and said, 'I see you are attached to that ugly jumper' I immediately slipped back into that familiar monastic silence and started groping inwardly for the synaptic snap it would take to enter placidity, grasping for it like someone plummeting to their death grasps for the parachute's ripcord. But she thundered around the flat and barked instructions at me at such a rapid rate it was impossible to achieve, and if I only nodded in reply she would sneer 'do you understand what I am asking' and when I started saying 'yes', 'okay', 'I can do that' she got bored of this too and told me, like she was speaking to a student or perhaps her own children, 'You are going to *have* to show some initiative'. A part of me had to accept that I deserved some of this brutality on account of having neglected this job so badly—she had the right to demand that I catch up on work I should have done already, and although I thought it was practically insane to speak to another human this way, in an attempt to maintain the determination I'd mustered over the weekend, I reminded myself that she had no other way of expressing herself. I'd had this thought before, so it was familiar ground, and always brought me to a kind of warm and familiar pity for Desdemona, that pathetic creature incapable of love or kindness, and this in turn allowed me to feel some superiority over her. Once I'd reached this emotional space, every following unkind word or degradation served to reinforce this silent conviction that my tolerance made me better than her in every way. It was a sophisticated mental trick that allowed me to avoid conflict of any kind.

It didn't stop me from running away, though. When she asked me to make her tea I was thrilled to discover she only had two teabags left. I shoved them into my bra and my ugly jumper was fortunately thick enough to conceal their addition. I told her she'd run out of tea and that I'd be happy to go out to buy more, and also, while I was at it, I would show some *initiative* and do a post office run. This bought me about 45 minutes of solitude, some of which I spent standing in an expensive perfume shop where I felt the scents move through me completely, as if I were made of mist.

As a mental exercise, hoping to reaffirm my moral superiority and fortify myself before I returned to her, I asked myself if I deserved to be spoken to the way Desdemona spoke to me. Instead of the desired smugness, the stark reality of the situation struck me and I immediately felt a wave of total shame followed by sadness. It seemed hopeless. I retreated instantly from the thought and told myself I had to grow up—I had to accept that this was just what being an adult was about, this is what life really is, and I had to confront this coldly and practically. If I'd resigned myself to working for Desdemona then this meant resigning myself to the full reality of this situation. I optimistically considered that there was even the possibility of me becoming so good at the job that she would no longer need to express disappointment in me. I invested great mental effort into imagining this outcome.

I left the perfume shop, which was a poor location for the mental turmoil I'd experienced in it, but I had to admit I'd cried in worse places.

Back in the flat I found her sitting on the sofa with her head tipped back. Her eyes were shut but her mouth was pursed with something resembling pain. The image was striking in the sense of privacy it exuded and for a split second, a memory of my mother, reclined in a hospital chair with her eyes shut as she received chemo from an IV drip, superimposed itself over Desdemona. There was a startling similarity. You should know that this doubling didn't open the door to sympathy—the feelings I'd had seeing my mother like that did not return to me then and they were not available to Desdemona. I just thought she looked sick.

She opened her eyes with a deep breath and invited me to sit next to her, which I did nervously.

'I think you should know there is some serious business happening…' she began, with a measured softness that I recognised was partly being deployed as an apology for her earlier behaviour.

I thought it was rich to describe any of the work she did as serious, frankly, but I simply nodded and said, 'Okay. What is it?'

'I—or really I mean the company, but really this does mean I—am being sued.'

For obvious reasons I cannot report the following part of the conversation and the practicalities of the case, nor can I comment on the culpability of anyone involved, but I can say that as Desdemona described the situation my first inclination was to determine whether or not *I* had any involvement in the situation, and whether the laxness I approached work with was about to get me testifying on a stand. I resolved with relief that this would not be required.

I knew very little about civil procedure on account of finding basically everything about it boring, so once she had finished her explanation about the cause for the suing, I asked, 'What does this mean, practically? Like, what's the process?'

A bolt of anger seemed to run through her and the force of it manifested in a very slight turn of her head towards me, and she stared at me from the corner of her eyes with what can only be described as derision.

'What happens is I get a good lawyer and I fuck them.'

I became distinctly aware of my pathetic little childish hands resting on my lap.

'Of course it is very expensive…' she continued. 'And costs will have to be cut.'

It was immediately obvious to me that I was the cost that was being cut and all my resolutions, the weekend of confronting my fears, my standing in the perfume shop and willing myself into adulthood, amounted to nothing. But instead of this manifesting into a feeling of defeat, a different feeling emerged.

That the impossibility of losing this job and its income—the total and physical fear of my life being reformed into something different against my will—had finally arrived should have crushed me entirely. But as I met her milky, probably inbred eyes and imagined never having to look at or speak to this woman again I experienced an incredible rush of relief. Every muscle in my body relaxed and I immediately began to consider my new and different life, which suddenly seemed promising and exciting. I could restart my master's, and do it well! I could go back to being a teaching assistant—the pay was barely enough to live on, but this was irrelevant, and everything I'd disliked about that job was unavailable to my mind in that moment. I imagined telling Normal Ben about this all and him cheering for me, telling me he was proud of me.

The relief was so significant it felt like a physical force and tears began to slide down my face involuntarily, with no accompanying sobbing. I noted, distantly, that these were genuine tears of pure joy, unalloyed with any other emotion.

'Oh no, my dear!' Desdemona leapt forward and snatched a tissue from the marble tissue box on her coffee table. I couldn't even imagine where one got a marble tissue box, and the fact that I would never have to ask myself a similar question about any of her ludicrous possessions again only increased the tears. 'No, no, my dear…' She handed me a bundle of tissues which I received in my hands, which seemed so adult now, and wiped my face.

'It's okay,' I said, 'it's okay. I'll figure something out. I know I'm not technically an employee, but will there be some kind of notice period or—'

'No, my dear, you have misunderstood. Please, do not worry…' she patted my knee, 'you are very safe.' Then she explained she was firing two of the account managers instead—their pay was much, much higher than mine, she noted with a chuckle, so the saving was more significant. 'In fact,' she said with a smile, 'I will need you more than ever.'

That I was already crying was convenient—with so little outward change, only I knew that my feelings were sliding from relief to despair. Desdemona believed the inverse, and seemed pleased to credit herself with the transformation.

•

When the PEACE method was first implemented in the UK it was taught to police officers who had been using their previous, more abusive and coercive methods for years. The new method was accompanied by a two-week training course. A year later a study showed that only a minority of officers were implementing the method correctly and that the majority had fallen back into their old habits. They would improve at implementing the method if they were being supervised, or were given a refreshment training course. It has been twenty years since the PEACE method was implemented. Presumably older methods are progressively dying out as older police officers retire. But who's to say. The cells in my body renew and I stay the same.

3.

Autumn began.

•

Normal Ben told me he'd come over after stopping by his friend Ant's 'antisocial-Thursday-night-birthday-drinks-but-not-party' party after work, and when he arrived he brought the bad weather in with him. He undid the several knots of his shoelaces and did not laugh as he usually did when I lurched to undo them. I asked how the party was. 'It was, um.' Then he stayed quiet.

I felt the earth's core, where the axis runs through it.

I promise, I promise, this all happened.

He sat on the chair next to my bed, a place he'd never sat before, and stared at the floor. In that honest, simple voice I'd come to recognise, he started speaking.

Until this moment, everything Normal Ben said to me I have reported to you as accurately as I can remember it. There will have been slippages, less significant moments where his language has not remained with me so I have invented substitutes and put them in quotation marks, but I have always endeavoured to represent the truth. I can't invent his language for the conversation that followed though—there are moments of the exchange that have stayed with me with glowing and knife-edged detail, and I can give you those, but for the rest I've had to draw the outlines, to make gestures and interpretations. I've done writers' tricks. But I know what happened that night and what I am telling you is true. You have no choice but to trust me.

'Isaac was there.'

He took a deep, steady breath.

'He knows Ant's sister. I don't know, I guess art school people all know each other. I tried to avoid him and then I told Ant I was going to leave and when he asked me why I said it's because,' he hesitated, 'I said it's because I don't talk to fucking rapists.'

Then I got confused by the story, with the list of names and people involved, both at the party and not, but I understood that Normal Ben's friend was disturbed, especially because of his sister's involvement, and then somehow more people got involved in this quiet exchange until Ant's sister, Sophie, joined and apparently she knew about me and pulled over Isaac himself.

'I didn't want to fucking talk to him. But we were all standing in Ant's kitchen and then Sophie got everyone to leave to "give us privacy" so then it was just the two of us and he started being like "bro, I get it" and I was like "I'm not your fucking bro" and he said this was all a misunderstanding, and he said he was sorry. He kept,' he shuddered, 'he kept saying that he wanted to apologise to you and that he hoped you were getting better, and that you got the help that you needed. He said that things between you got "toxic", but he said he never hurt you. He got…' and here Normal Ben had the shyness and embarrassment men sometimes have when something is serious so he said this bit casually, like he was dismissing the sentence: 'He got really emotional. And said that he could never do something like that and he didn't know why you'd say he had.' Then he said Isaac took out his phone and showed him messages I'd sent, messages that were friendly, needy, flirty, messages that were less than a year old, and that Isaac asked if those were the kind of messages I'd send if he'd done what I was saying he'd done and then apparently he said, several times, that it 'doesn't add up' and after Normal Ben repeated that phrase he leant his head into his hands and cradled it as I stayed silent.

From the cradle of his hands he said he told Isaac to fuck off and then he left, and that he was embarrassed about having caused a scene, that he'd never done anything like that before, but he felt it was the right thing to do. But he wasn't sure now. He kept thinking about things. And he worried that maybe, maybe he'd got things wrong.

'I know you've had a hard life. And I know I can't understand all of it. Like, I don't know what it feels like to have your mum die and I think it'll fucking kill me when mine does, and—' his sentence became garbled as he said several times that he couldn't even think about the idea of his mother dying, that it was too painful, and then he said that he felt, sometimes, that I didn't trust him to understand me, so I exaggerated stories about my life, but he forgave this because he thought I just needed him to listen, 'to pay attention to you, because maybe you feel like no one else does.'

He said that sometimes he felt frightened of hurting me. That he'd started getting worried before we had sex because he wasn't sure if he would do something wrong, and that for the first time in his life he'd realised how much potential he had to hurt someone. That it felt like everyone he'd known in his life up until me just managed to live life so easily, even with heartbreak and misery, that even his friends on antidepressants seemed to cope. He said it seemed like things had more consequence to me. That nothing was ever insignificant. And that he also admired this in some way. That it meant I was so passionate, so focused on what I cared about, and that he'd also never known anyone to care so much about small things, to argue so intensely about politics or inequality, nor anyone who was so persuasive when she argued. But that he felt like sometimes that conviction meant there was no space for him to have a different opinion than mine, that I always needed him to agree with what I was saying, and that he'd never really worried about this in any serious way until tonight. That he wished this wasn't true, but that he had wondered if Isaac might have been telling the truth. If I might have lied. That he felt horrible for admitting that. That it was the worst thing he'd ever thought.

He said, 'I don't know what to believe, Aea. I feel so stupid. I feel so, so stupid.'

He made eye contact with me for the first time since he'd arrived. He would have found my face controlled and still.

It does not seem fair that I, alone, am now allowed to repeat and litigate the conversation that happened between me and Normal Ben that night, but nor does it seem fair that he got to invent what may or may not have been the most traumatic event of my life and repeat it to a room full of strangers.

I think I said, 'I'm sorry you've had a hard night. I don't know what I would have done in your position. But I wish you hadn't spoken to Isaac. I wish you hadn't said anything.' I may not have said it as elegantly, but this is essentially what I said.

What I wanted to say was that I thought I was too special to have bad things happen to me. That bad things only happened to people who couldn't see them coming—ordinary people who were less perceptive, less intelligent than I am, and I wanted to tell him that the greatest injury in my life was the repeated reminder that I was just like everyone else: that I would grieve, that I would suffer, that I would be hurt just like every other idiot, and that each of these events was telling me, bragging to me: you are normal, you are normal, you are normal. And despite every effort I doubted

I would ever learn my lesson or change. I wanted to say that I would always think that I could outsmart any punishing outcome by designing myself just right, and I wanted to say that I would hate the person who proved me wrong every time. And I hated him. I hated him. I hated him. I felt that he thought he knew me better than I did, that he understood the world better than I could. And the fact was that no matter what, I would always think he was too stupid to actually get it right because he was stupid enough to trust me, and I would always, always think he was stupid for applying his shallow, lazy, inherited understanding of the world onto me so that I would become a person he could understand: an attention-seeking woman, someone who needed him. I wanted to hurt him. I wanted to make him feel small. But more than that, more than any of these other parts, I wanted him to believe me, and I knew what this would take.

So I said, I think, 'I don't know what I would call what happened between me and Isaac, but it seems like you do, so let's run through it together and why don't you tell me what it was,' and then I told him what happened. I described all the details leading up to that night, I unfolded the weeks surrounding it, I told him what I felt was my responsibility, what I felt was Isaac's, I told him about the argument we'd had, I told him I'd broken up with Isaac even though I loved him, I did not acknowledge but registered that he flinched at the mention of me having loved another man, I recited the words Issac and I had used, I told him how I'd sat on my fucking knees and held Isaac's hands, looked him in the eye and told him I loved him but that this had to stop, that I had to go, I told him what Isaac did in return, which was kiss me, I told him why I felt like I couldn't just leave the room, that I wanted to, that I didn't, I told him what we'd drunk earlier, how much, I imitated Isaac's mocking laugh when I said he was being unkind, I imitated how he'd called me stupid, I described the furniture in Isaac's room, I described the configuration of our bodies, I described how Isaac and I usually had sex, I told him what parts I usually liked and what parts I tolerated, I described what was different this time, which wasn't very much, I told him what I remembered Isaac saying, which was demeaning, as usual, I told him what I remembered feeling, which was very little, I told him what I remembered saying, which was nothing at all. I unspooled every detail for him like a police report. I said that the next day I'd realised how little I remembered of it all, I told him how I decided to forget about it, I told him that a feeling lingered and two months later I'd been standing in Tesco buying a pear when I realised that I felt like I'd been holding my breath for two months. I told him that it was that same moment that I realised I'd still been in love with Isaac and that I'd wondered when that feeling would leave. I asked him if he could make sense of that? I didn't let him answer. I asked him if he knew what that felt like? I didn't let him speak. I told him I changed my mind about what had happened each time I thought about it.

I told him that if the sex was identical to all our other sex then the only variation will have been Isaac's intention. And I couldn't know what Isaac had intended. I couldn't know, so it was up to me to decide what had happened. That I didn't know what word to use to describe it. That the truth was that I didn't know if there was a word for this kind of injury, nor a way to hold people to account for it. And then I said, 'So, what would you call that?' And I watched his face shift through a succession of minor but perceptible gear changes—his frontalis trembled, his depressor anguli oris seized, his mentalis was activated—which could mean anything, anything at all, but if I had to guess, I would say he was experiencing shame, anger, pain, to varying degrees simultaneously and I resented that he could look at my face and come to his own conclusion which I was certain would be wrong, but there was still some softness, a droop of pity around his mouth, as he said, 'That's not how you described it before' with a kindness that was an invitation for me to see things from his point of view, which I simply did not want to do, so instead I said, 'Why would I have told you any of that before? It's none of your business. Why would I have told you something so fucking embarrassing. Do you know how humiliating it is to love a person you hate?' and it is very rare that a single sentence can render the world into such painful clarity, but as soon as I'd asked the question I felt the room's edges harden and he said, 'No. No, I don't,' like he was trying to convince himself and then he said that I'd told him I'd avoided sex for a while after Isaac, that I'd said the relationship had shown me the depth of how people could hurt each other and this was partly why I'd been so resistant to Normal Ben's affection, why I sometimes still looked sceptical when he was nice to me, and as he said all this he got more energised and his volume increased and he said, 'But I asked you, about the case, and... I asked you and you said nothing' and I said, 'What was I supposed to say? You'd already made your mind up, you didn't care what I had to say' and then he asked, 'If that was all true then what else was I supposed to assume?' and I said, 'I don't know' and then he asked again so I shrugged an antagonising, jerking shrug and he said, even louder, nearly shouting, 'No—tell me, what was I *supposed* to believe?' and then inhaled sharply, practically gasped at the sound of his own voice, at the idea that he was angry, and began to pace the room and seemed to be about to cry or shout, and there were several points throughout this conversation where I cried and this was one of them, as I tried to comfort him, at first pragmatically and then pleadingly, to try and make him feel better for nearly losing his temper, a thing I was sure had only happened a handful of times in his life, and then I cried as I said that I didn't know what he wanted from me, and the tears unexpectedly pitched into sobs as I said a rotation of 'I don't have an answer', 'I don't know what to say', 'I don't know, I don't know, I don't know what you want from me' and then he had no choice but to comfort me, to wrap me up and let the attack pass, and an idle and rational part of me thought that everything he'd said had been true, I had said those things about Isaac, and what had I wanted him to believe? How could I possibly imagine there was any ambiguity there? And then I thought about how every decision and action in my life, everything I'd done or had done to me, was the result of a thousand commingled feelings and desires and actions that were both my fault and the fault of others, my fault for being fascinated by the possibility of being hurt and perhaps enjoying the cusp of it too, and that in trying to make Normal Ben be kind to me, in trying to make him see the part of me that liked and feared my pain, I'd either attached the story to a comprehensible thing like the vast and destructive force a single man had represented in my life or allowed him to make the association himself, and the fact he'd fully believed it in his blunt and simple way was not his fault but mine for letting him, and as I thought this another part of me, the small, rabbit-brained and frantic, heart-thumping part, imagined lying down in the snow until my heart stopped, imagined driving into a tree and my sternum collapsing into the steering wheel, imagined gasping in water at the bottom of a canal, imagined diving from a building and feeling my skull erupt, imagined getting tangled and divided by the wheels of a train, imagined a bolt of electricity punching through me, imagined a dressing gown belt crushing my larynx shut, imagined the rolling spasms after a fistful of pills, imagined leaping from a bridge and shattering feet-first, imagined stabbing me in the jugular and emptying onto a pavement, imagined bursting through a windshield and being shaved to bone by asphalt, imagined every way I could take matters into my own hands, every way to assert control over my life, and then I looked at Normal Ben and thought that I would be taught again and again, no matter what, that the course of my life would be determined by someone other than me, and suddenly the idea that I should strive to be a good person, pure and honest, seemed childishly stupid, it seemed comically naive, and as he held my hands and kissed my forehead, tucked my hair behind my ears and did the gestures that were so familiar by now they seemed to emerge from him almost involuntarily, I pictured him at seven years old, sitting on the sofa and leaning against his mother as he watched TV feeling so grateful for her presence, I pictured him alone in his bedroom, facing a mounting anger as he heard his parents argue and did nothing to defend her, I pictured him as a normal teenager, attracted to girls and frightened of them, I pictured him falling in love with his first girlfriend, I pictured him having sex with her in his student accommodation single bed and them sleeping effortlessly intertwined, I pictured him having an argument with a man in a club who'd groped her, I pictured him feeling good about himself as he comforted her, I pictured him in their first flat in London together, I pictured them in the kitchen as she told him she didn't love him anymore, I pictured his life crumbling in that moment and him realising for the first time that he could fall victim to people's capricious ways, I pictured how his unwavering respect for her had acted as a life raft, how it had allowed him to forgive her and make sense of his sadness, how he knew she wouldn't have done it unless she needed to, I imagined what he was feeling now, sitting across from me, and I realised that this was probably one of the worst moments in Normal Ben's life and it was thanks to me, and the surge of pity came, and I cried for him instead of me, and the surge of guilt came, and I cried my shame out, and he started saying that he didn't want to tell me 'how to describe' my trauma, and I wanted to tell him that he should because maybe I didn't want to decide anymore, and he said that he thought I should 'maybe see a therapist' and for a moment it seemed like this was the way out of this conversation—this thing we both wanted to end more than anything—and that we could delegate whatever was wrong with me to some professional and pretend that what was happening in my bedroom, this destruction of what we knew about each other, was separate from our real lives, and I thought of how one of the first studies into pathological lying was conducted in 1906 and concluded that there is no real treatment, that the condition is akin to an addiction and should be treated like one, so the patient is encouraged to redirect their 'linguistic powers' to something more productive, like writing, and Normal Ben asked again if I thought I should see a therapist and extended this way out for both of us and I nearly took it before a thought crossed my mind, which was why this conversation was happening in the first place, then the thought that it was incredibly unfair, wrong, that the way I described one event in my life should determine so much of how I should be treated, that after everything I'd told him, all the blatant lies, it would come down to this, to me deciding if I was a victim or not to determine what kind of kindness I received from Normal Ben or from anyone else, and then the thought that it was incredibly unfair that my life could be flattened so easily, that despite my every effort to be complex, creative and nasty this could be taken away from me instantly, and the thought that it was unfair to Normal Ben also came, unfair that as I looked at him and saw this normal man who seemed to be doing his best I also saw a representation of this flattening, I saw the world rendered simple, so instead of taking the way out he'd offered and instead of explaining any of this to him I simply said, 'I think you're being sexist,' and his face coloured and hardened and he said, 'Why?' and I said he was projecting onto me, I told him that I thought he still couldn't understand why I enjoyed sex or why I behaved the way I did I told him that he thought of me as weaker than I actually am I told him that he thought sexual violence was an inevitability in women's lives and in doing so was perpetuating rape culture I told him that in believing in conventional narratives of rape he excluded a thousand variations of violence that didn't belong to a black and white thinking I told him that I didn't know what I would call what happened between me and Isaac but instead of believing this, instead of asking me, tonight Normal Ben walked into a kitchen and made a decision for me. I told him, 'Now I have to decide whether I agree with you or not, and no matter what I say I will be lying.' There is a lot that he could have said to this and there is a lot that he should have said. But he couldn't, he simply couldn't, because I began to cry so completely and so violently that our world's edges frayed. I watched Normal Ben unravel, weak-jointed and exhausted, into a wet-eyed heap. I expected him to leave. And I wanted him to. But instead he pawed forward, meekly, asked if he could touch me, if he could be near me, if he could hold me, please. And I said yes, yes, yes. And he held me hard. And he apologised again. And he apologised again. And he said that he believed me. And he did. He did. He promised.

•

He believed me.

•

He promised.

•

He promised.

•

He did.

•

In the morning, before leaving for work, he asked if I could forgive him.

•

Tugging his shoelaces with my toes, I said I could.

I do.

I promised.

4.

Winter.

•

We took our normal route through Battersea Park, swearing about errant cyclists and dismissing the advances of hungry geese. There was no snow, but enough frost that our footsteps left a mark. The moment I'd expected him to take my hand, Normal Ben asked where I had found the body.

I led him to the spot and pointed at the dirt, where the passage of death had left no trace.

He looked at the ground reverently, then scanned the houses with windows within view. 'No one even noticed,' he said quietly. 'It's horrible. No one even noticed him out here.'

I watched his face's performance of a grief he had no right to. After a moment he asked if we could leave. I nodded and gestured for him to lead the way, then stepped over the body to follow behind.

AEA VARFIS-VAN WARMELO is a British Greek writer living in London. She is the author of *Intellectual Property*, a pamphlet of poems.

Graywolf Press publishes risk-taking, visionary writers who transform culture through literature. As a nonprofit organization, Graywolf relies on the generous support of its donors to bring books like this one into the world.

This publication is made possible, in part, by the voters of Minnesota through a Minnesota State Arts Board Operating Support grant, thanks to a legislative appropriation from the arts and cultural heritage fund. Significant support has also been provided by other generous contributions from foundations, corporations, and individuals. To these supporters we offer our heartfelt thanks.

The text of *Attention-Seeking Behavior*
is set in Adobe Garamond.
Composition by Geethik Technologies.
Manufactured by Sheridan on acid-free,
30 percent postconsumer wastepaper.